The gunner adjus
and seemed to he

"Look out!" Donna screamed.

Bolan snapped around in time to see a big man setting himself and taking aim with a .357 revolver.

The warrior threw himself to the pavement and rolled, followed by a line of slugs that gouged holes in the ground behind him. Bolan jumped to his feet, his Beretta up and tracking.

The big West Virginian didn't get a second chance to take out the Executioner. A three-round burst slammed into his chest and he sank to his knees, dropping his weapon.

Bolan was already moving as Malik fired his weapon. He was no marksman, and his three rounds cracked through a nearby plate-glass window.

The Executioner's second volley hit the Arab squarely in the face, the bullets coring his brain. Two up, two down.

Bolan grabbed the petrified Donna Dow by the arm. "Time to go." The sharks were circling, and the numbers were falling fast.

DON PENDLETON'S
THE EXECUTIONER®
FEATURING MACK BOLAN®

STEEL AND FLAME

A GOLD EAGLE BOOK FROM
WORLDWIDE.
TORONTO · NEW YORK · LONDON · PARIS
AMSTERDAM · STOCKHOLM · HAMBURG
ATHENS · MILAN · TOKYO · SYDNEY

First edition March 1992

ISBN 0-373-61159-5

Special thanks and acknowledgment to
Carl Furst for his contribution to this work.

STEEL AND FLAME

In doing what we ought, we deserve no praise,
because it is our duty.

—St. Augustine
354–430

I've always been a soldier first and last.
I made a vow to fight for those who couldn't
fight back themselves. To stand on the sidelines just
isn't my style.

—Mack Bolan

THE
MACK BOLAN®
LEGEND

Nothing less than a war could have fashioned the destiny of the man called Mack Bolan. Bolan earned the Executioner title in the jungle hell of Vietnam.

But this soldier also wore another name—Sergeant Mercy. He was so tagged because of the compassion he showed to wounded comrades-in-arms and Vietnamese civilians.

Mack Bolan's second tour of duty ended prematurely when he was given emergency leave to return home and bury his family, victims of the Mob. Then he declared a one-man war against the Mafia.

He confronted the Families head-on from coast to coast, and soon a hope of victory began to appear. But Bolan had broken society's every rule. That same society started gunning for this elusive warrior—to no avail.

So Bolan was offered amnesty to work within the system against terrorism. This time, as an employee of Uncle Sam, Bolan became Colonel John Phoenix. With a command center at Stony Man Farm in Virginia, he and his new allies—Able Team and Phoenix Force—waged relentless war on a new adversary: the KGB.

But when his one true love, April Rose, died at the hands of the Soviet terror machine, Bolan severed all ties with Establishment authority.

Now, after a lengthy lone-wolf struggle and much soul-searching, the Executioner has agreed to enter an "arm's-length" alliance with his government once more, reserving the right to pursue personal missions in his Everlasting War.

PROLOGUE

Interstate 77 originates in Cleveland and runs south to Columbia, South Carolina. Carrying traffic both ways, the highway is an important link between America's industrial heartland and the South. At Marietta, Ohio, Interstate 77 crosses the Ohio River to West Virginia on a new bridge built specifically to carry it.

Or it did until terror struck.

The towboat *Grove City* was moving downriver, pushing eighteen barges with twenty-five thousand tons of structural steel. The current increased speed by about twenty percent, the vessel moving at a steady fourteen knots. Somewhere between Willow Island Lock and Dam and the bridge that was a part of Interstate 77, *Grove City*'s routine run took a frightening turn.

The towboat was boarded by a gang of seven heavily armed men. Moving with well-rehearsed efficiency, the gunmen immediately split up. Half of them rounded up the startled crew from below deck. Without any chance to resist, the men were then herded onto the barge nearest the towboat and held there under the guns of four masked men.

At the same time, three other masked men, one un-armed, moved quickly toward the pilothouse. The two armed men flung the door open and aimed their mini-Uzis to the startled pilot's chest. The man threw his hands into the air, and without a word he was marched to the barge with the rest of his crew.

The hijackers had needed less than four minutes to take control of the *Grove City*.

Under the helm of the assailants, the towboat con-tinued on its course toward the Interstate 77 bridge. Supported by concrete and steel piers, the bridge is an imposing structure. An island lies in the river at a point before the span, narrowing the channel, thus making it more difficult to navigate.

But the masked pilot knew his business. He guided the long, heavy tow through the tricky passage and shoved in his throttles as the *Grove City* approached the bridge. On the barge, the horrified crew saw what was coming and threw themselves onto the deck.

As the rightmost lead barge slammed into the bridge pier with a thunderous roar, it ruptured immediately and took on enough water to sink. The cables holding the barges in formation snapped and flew as the mo-mentum of tens of thousands of tons of tow and cargo placed insurmountable pressure on the pier. The next barge overrode the first and slammed into the pier with another booming crash.

The second collision was more than the bridge could sustain. Concrete crumbled, riveted joints tore apart and heavy girders twisted like tinfoil as steel from the superstructure began to fall.

The collapse was slow. As the Ohio side of the bridge crumbled and began to fall into the river, cars screeched to a halt. Others sped off the far side before the road disappeared beneath them. Two truck drivers were unable to do either and found the roadway disintegrating in front of them. Blind with fear, they jumped from their cabs and ran back to safety, just before they saw their trucks and four lanes of roadway disappear into the river.

The masked gunmen hadn't waited to see what would happen. By the time the bridge fell, they were in a power speedboat and were racing away on the dark river to a rendezvous with a nearby van that would carry them far from the disaster before anyone could muster pursuit.

With no one at the wheel, the *Grove City* spun on the current, cables still snapping. Before the pilot could make it back to his controls, the big towboat was slipping sideways downstream, its diesels still pushing six or seven barges into the muddy bank. One of these held the shaken, but not seriously injured crew. The tow and barges finally snagged on the debris of the bridge and were hung up there until the pilot reached the pilothouse and reversed the engines.

1

"The river was blocked for a week while the wreckage was pulled out of the channel. It's a small miracle that nobody was killed."

Mack Bolan sat grim-faced through a briefing in a conference room in the main building of Stony Man Farm. The report wasn't good.

"It was a warning," Hal Brognola continued, "to show us what they can do. About fifteen percent of the nation's domestic commerce moves on the Mississippi and its tributaries. That's almost six hundred million tons of cargo every year. What would it do to this country if that traffic was suddenly stopped, say, for a whole year?"

Bolan shook his head. "How can they do that?"

"They can't. Not all at once, anyway. But take the Ohio River. A tremendous amount of shipping moves on it. And it's vulnerable. The river isn't deep enough to carry all of the traffic, so it's dammed at intervals, all the way from Pittsburgh to Cairo. The traffic has to go through locks and... You begin to get the picture."

Bolan nodded. "Destroy just one of those locks and you'd block the river."

"Maybe worse. The dammed water would gush through a damaged lock from thirty miles upstream. It could do flood damage like the valley has never seen before."

"Or suppose they blew a dam," Bolan suggested.

"That'd take a carload of explosives, but we can't dismiss it as a possibility."

The Executioner nodded gravely. He also had seen too much in the hellgrounds to rule out anything. "That leaves the big question. Who?"

"A group called the Green and Black," Brognola said. "At least that's how they sign themselves."

"You've heard from them?"

"The President has heard from them."

"What do they want?"

"Start with an unreasonable amount of money—millions," Brognola replied. "That's what they call their 'first demand.' After that, they'll let us know."

"Of course we're not paying."

"You're damned right we're not paying," Brognola said, red-faced with anger. He reached into his shirt pocket to grab a cigar, thought about it, then put it back. "I'd like to send in the whole first team."

"I work alone."

"I knew you'd say that. All I ask is that you keep in touch."

"Have we got anything else to go on?"

The big Fed took a deep breath. "The truth is, Striker, that our intel is limited. These guys are trained pros, there's no doubt about it. But we don't know how they organize themselves, or where they hide out. There's something, though. For the past several months, there's been a surge in drug activity along the river, where little has existed before."

"So you figure the Green and Black could be financing their operation by pushing dope?" Bolan knew it wouldn't be the first time that international criminals had parlayed narcotics into grander schemes of terror.

"It's possible. Hell, it's the best we've got to go on right now. We'll put you on one of the river towboats and you can make your own assessment. But it's vital that we trade intel. Otherwise it's your play. The President said to remind you of that. And he said to use your own methods, and your own judgment. There'll be no questions asked."

"ANYTHING THAT FLOATS," the pilot said. "*Anything*. That could be them."

Mack Bolan stood beside the pilot; watching him maneuver a long string of barges up the dark river. To the river pilot he was Mike Belasko, a security man for the towboat company. That was why the pilot talked easily to him, telling him things he might not have told anyone else.

"As much as I wish it weren't so, there's no way you can keep everything away from your tow. I've got forty men aboard. Half of them I know pretty well, the other half I don't. If one of them is out there pickin' up junk, he could easily get past me."

The pilot's name was Doyle Tolliver. He was also the captain of the towboat, which was named *Henry J. Muldoon*, and had been working the river for over twenty years. Bolan recognized the frustration in the man's voice and judged him sincere.

Although Bolan had been on the towboat for only a couple of hours, he could see that what Tolliver had been saying was true. A small boat could pull alongside the *Henry J. Muldoon* in the darkness, hand a package to a crewman on board and nobody in the wheelhouse would notice.

Compounding the problem was the fact that a tow like the *Henry J. Muldoon* and its fifteen barges didn't stop along the river to take on fuel, groceries or other supplies. Fuel barges moved alongside the big boat and pumped thousands of gallons of diesel fuel into the vessel's huge tanks without interrupting its journey.

As well, small boats came alongside to deliver groceries and mail. Still others came to deliver videotapes, magazines, tobacco and—though company rules forebade it—beer and whisky.

"We're like a little floating town," Tolliver said. "What control do I have over what comes on and off?"

Little, the Executioner thought, but if anybody tried to make a narcotics drop tonight, he'd be ready. In the meantime, Bolan was learning as much as he could.

The truth was that piloting was an exact and demanding science. Though the water was three-quarters of a mile wide, riverbank to riverbank, only a narrow channel was deep enough for the barges. In some places along their route, the channel ran along the Kentucky shore; in others it was closer to the Ohio shore.

Even with navigation lights if Tolliver lost his concentration and let the *Henry J. Muldoon* wander outside the channel, the lead barges could easily run aground on gravel bars that at places extended hundreds of yards into the river. But the pilot knew his job and guided the tow back and forth across the river as necessary.

The pilothouse was dark except for the dim glow from instruments—green from the radar screen, orange from the sonar depth finder, yellowish from the faces of a dozen gauges. From time to time Tolliver switched on powerful arc lights that were fixed to the roof of the pilothouse, stabbing the night with long, narrow beams that illuminated anything that might have caught either man's attention.

"Never saw much drugs in this part of the country before," Tolliver said. "I mean, there's always been people that got hold of it some way and made fools of themselves on the stuff. But nowadays..." He stopped and shook his head. "You take a girl who two, three years ago wanted nothing more than to win a baton-twirling contest. Right now she's laying around shot up on some kind of stuff with nothing more on her mind than where's she going to get her next hit. It's pitiful, Mike. I tell you, it's pitiful."

Bolan silently agreed. He'd seen the same thing a hundred times over. A less determined man might have been discouraged. But it only made the Executioner stronger in his resolve to do something about it.

Cocaine and heroin were reaching the Ohio Valley in massive quantities, destroying the quality of life in its small towns. If the Green and Black was responsible, then he'd just have to take the organization out of the play.

Tolliver couldn't guess the thoughts of the steely-eyed man beside him, however, and he continued. "I figure the reason you're on this boat, Mike, is either because of the drugs, or what happened at Burkett Island."

"I never heard of Burkett Island."

Captain Tolliver turned his face away from the river for a moment, and in the glow from the radar screen Bolan could see the skepticism on his face. Then he turned back to the river and said nothing.

Tolliver switched on a spotlight and manipulated the beam so it focused on a navigation light a half mile away. He then pulled in his right rudder lever, and the giant tow began a slow swing toward the beacon.

"Sometimes the current drags the buoys downstream a ways, which screws up your steering," Tolliver explained. "That's what happened at Burkett Island. I'd been coming downstream pretty fast, steering on a buoy that had moved a hundred yards in the last four hours. So I fetched up on a gravel bar. I mean she crunched into that bar with one hell of a whack. And you know what happened."

"No, I guess I don't. What happened?"

"Most of the deckhands threw themselves on their bellies. Three jumped overboard, because they knew what was going to happen. The tow started to twist, and the cables that link the barges together broke. When one of them things break, it's like a whip. Worse. It's like a knife. If a man's standing there when it whips across the deck, it'll cut him in two. One guy,

Grady, did just that. And I mean it cut him in two! I'd heard of it, but I'd never seen it happen in all my years on the river."

Tolliver shook his head. He switched on all his searchlights and had a quick look at the water ahead, then switched them off again. Bolan had learned that pilots used their lights as little as possible, because the glare contracted their pupils and impaired their night vision. The warrior could relate to that wisdom.

"They did an autopsy," the captain continued, "and Grady was full of heroin. Stoned out of his mind, as they say. I figure he'd have jumped like the other guys if he hadn't been."

Bolan had told the truth when he said he hadn't heard of the Burkett Island incident. However, he'd heard the rest of it—riverboat crews were shooting and sniffing.

A bright red spot appeared suddenly on Doyle Tolliver's face. It was just below his ear, on the rear of his jaw. Bolan threw himself on the pilot and knocked him to the deck, just as the pilothouse resounded with the crack of a heavy, high-velocity slug.

"Son of a bitch!" the captain yelled.

Bolan had drawn the .44 Magnum Desert Eagle and sprung to a combat stance. He was momentarily surprised. There was no glass on the floor, and the side window wasn't broken—bulletproof glass. The pilot had been in no real danger.

Bolan scanned the bank for the rifleman. It was dark, and he could have been anywhere—behind a tree, in the leafy brush. But more than likely he was gone.

"Thanks, Mike," Tolliver said as he struggled up and resumed his place between the steering levers. "We put bulletproof glass in all the pilothouses years ago, before this drugs business came along. During the strikes awhile back, a few guys tried to put bullets through some of the scabs."

Tolliver tried to appear cool about a rifleman on the riverbank taking a potshot at him, but Bolan saw his hands trembling on the steering levers. Bulletproof glass or no, a man on a towboat on the river was an easy target for a sniper with a rifle on the bank. If a gunman really wanted to take a pilot out, he'd do it.

"How did you know about the sniper?"

Bolan returned the Desert Eagle to its leather. "Red spot on the side of your face where somebody was aiming. Who'd want to kill you?"

Tolliver turned down the corners of his mouth and shook his head slowly. "Nobody wants to kill me." He picked up his microphone and reported the incident to other pilots up and down the river.

"It doesn't figure," Bolan insisted. "Do you think the rifleman knew he couldn't put a shot through that glass and—"

"Figured he'd just scare the hell out of me? Well, he did a damned good job."

"Has anybody been hit on any of the other boats?" Bolan asked.

"No, not that I know of. Maybe all they got in mind is scaring us," Tolliver suggested, trying hard to convince himself. "Yeah. Maybe that's all they got in mind."

AFTER THE TOWBOAT had traveled a few miles down-stream, Bolan left the pilothouse and went below into the galley. He sat down and was served a cup of coffee by Lisa, a big Scandinavian woman who ran the kitchen. Two deckhands came in. "Mike Belasko" was, as far as they knew, a company cop, and there-fore someone to be avoided. Bolan had hoped to strike up a conversation with some of the crew, but one look at the cold stares from these two told him instantly that he'd learn nothing from them.

After drinking his coffee, Bolan went up on deck. He stood just outside the pilothouse door for a few minutes, letting his eyes get accustomed to the dark-ness. Then he walked forward and stepped over onto one of the barges.

A man had to be careful walking the barges at night. Their decks were a tangle of pipes and cargo. Al-though cables lashed the clumsy vessels together, there was still considerable shifting. As well, except for the navigation lights at the front of the tow, the barges were dark. One wrong step and a person could easily fall overboard into the river, without anybody in the pilothouse noticing.

The warrior was aware of this, and of the vulnera-bility of exposure on the barges' low flat hulls, so he moved carefully. Walking forward, stepping from one barge to the next, Bolan was soon several hundred feet in front of *Henry J. Muldoon*. If, as Tolliver had sug-gested, drops were being made, Bolan would be the first one to know about it.

The river wasn't entirely dark. Lights burned on both banks, in towns and in farmhouses. Cars moved

on the roads along the river, their headlights sometimes sweeping out over the water. The tow passed
close to the Kentucky shore as it rounded a bend, and
Bolan could see three fishermen silhouetted in the light
of a kerosene lantern. They waved at the big towboat
as it passed, and Tolliver favored them with a short
honk of the boat's loud horn.

The small boats on the river were either skiffs,
powered by outboards, or what the older men on the
river called johnboats. Flat on both ends and drawing
very little water, a johnboat was easy to row. It was an
ideal boat for fishing. It was also ideal for moving
across the dark river when you didn't want to be noticed.

Bolan decided he'd seen all he could by walking on
the barges and turned to walk back to the *Muldoon*.

As he neared the barge immediately in front of and
to the portside of the towboat, a noise caught his attention. It sounded like a voice—at a time and place
where no voice should have been heard. Bolan's combat instincts tingled. Like a big cat, the Executioner
stealthily followed the noise to its source.

"Watch out! Company cop out on the tow some-
wheres!"

Bolan couldn't see the man behind that warning,
but it sounded as if the voice came from over the
barge's side. Then he heard a faint thump, which he
took for the sound of a wooden boat bumping against
the side of the barge's steel hull.

Bolan drew the Desert Eagle and began to make his
way forward. After a minute or so, he saw the vague
shadows of two men, maybe three, in a boat along-

side the barge. He glanced around. If it was indeed a drug drop, the men in the boat had to be meeting somebody.

"Back off! We can't do it! The son of a bitch is out here someplace."

Although the voice had come from no more than twenty feet away, Bolan couldn't see the man. No doubt he was on the same deck, hiding among the complex of fat pipes. The guy's warning hadn't discouraged the men in the boat. Watching their shadows—still blurry against the darkness of the river and its banks—Bolan saw that one of them had climbed aboard the tow.

Tolliver obviously had no idea that he had a trespasser on board, or he could have blinded them with the beams of his arc lamps.

But ahead on the Ohio shore was something just as good. Light. It came from the dock of a marina, and as the tow moved upstream, the men in the little boat were going to be silhouetted against that glow of light.

He waited.

The *Muldoon*'s tow moved slowly, eventually reaching the position Bolan had expected, and the men—three of them—were distinctly silhouetted.

Bolan had chosen his position carefully, so as to offer nothing but shadows to the men in the boat, or on deck.

"The company cop is over here, fellows."

They didn't hesitate. An automatic weapon spit a stream of slugs in the direction of where they'd heard the voice. A pistol barked twice, and the man who'd boarded the barge let fly a shotgun blast.

The gunfire missed its target, as Bolan had moved immediately after speaking. As he'd hoped, their muzzle-flashes made them targets.

Bolan fired the Desert Eagle at the spot where he'd seen the flame of the automatic weapon, then rolled to his right.

He couldn't tell if he'd gotten a hit, but the Desert Eagle's thunder had gotten their attention. With a yell, one man jumped back into the boat, and Bolan heard him drop heavily to the bottom.

The Executioner had all three men pinned down in the johnboat, and he moved in. They had apparently thrown a rope around something on the barge and were being towed along. The man with the automatic lay dead on the bottom of the johnboat, his gun still in hand, as the pistolman tried frantically to cut the rope free.

Standing cover for his buddy, the shotgunner made an easy target. Bolan took him out with a head shot that left him dead before he hit the water.

The surviving hardguy had had enough. Having seen his two friends go down, he jumped into the dark water. Bolan fired once but couldn't be sure if he hit him, because they were moving downstream.

That took care of the threat from the boat. Bolan cut it away and turned his attention to the rear. The man who'd cried the warning was still a deadly threat. If possible, Bolan wanted to take him alive.

But as he worked his way across the barge toward the *Henry J. Muldoon*, Bolan realized that whoever had been out to meet the johnboat was now gone.

BOLAN PICKED UP TWO CUPS of coffee and returned to the pilothouse. Doyle Tolliver stood at the wheel, trying hard to look calm.

"I suppose that's what you're here for," he said to the warrior. Both his expression and tone of voice made it difficult for Bolan to tell if he meant the coffee, or the gunfight out on the tow.

"I didn't see anything, did you?" Bolan asked. He'd just as soon not be asked to explain why two or three dead men were floating on the river near a boat that probably also carried some envelopes of white powder. "I thought it was dead quiet out there."

Tolliver nodded. "Yeah. Dead quiet. A quiet night."

Bolan sipped coffee. "You've got somebody on board I want to talk to."

2

It was after two in the morning when the turboprop landed at the Noble County Airport near Caldwell, Ohio. The aircraft's flight had originated in El Paso, Texas, and had made one refueling stop before its arrival.

The airport had been chosen because it was deserted at this time of night. The runway lights had been switched on by a radio signal only at the last moment, when the pilot needed them. With any luck at all, no one would notice the landing.

Having turned off the landing lights, the turboprop taxied quickly back to the ramp, where it was met by a black Mercedes. A heavyset man accepted the hand of the driver, who helped him step down from the plane. A third man carried luggage from the airplane to the car in two quick trips. Two minutes later, the Mercedes drove away from the airport.

The pilot taxied to the end of the runway and, within four minutes of landing, the plane was airborne again. The turboprop's shrieking engines woke half the population of the village of Caldwell and brought the town's only on-duty policeman to the airport to see what was going on.

By that time, the Mercedes was well on its way down Interstate 77. Outside of Marietta, traffic was diverted because of the collapsed bridge. This brought a smug grin to the face of the heavyset man. It was the only time he could remember not minding a delay.

In the city of Marietta, a suite had been reserved in the Lafayette Hotel. The heavyset man checked in, signing the registration card as Benjamin Johnson, President, Mahoney Petroleum, Incorporated. The large, silent man who had carried his bags was registered as Frank Gunther.

As the men went up to their suite, the clerk picked up the telephone, woke the town's mayor and breathlessly told her that the oilman from Texas had checked in. She was glad to hear it. The town could use some new excitement in the Ohio and West Virginia oilfields.

Although it was the best the hotel had to offer, Benjamin Johnson wasn't satisfied with the suite. It was, in fact, the best accommodation available for many miles around. But it wasn't to the taste of a man who was accustomed to suites at five-star hotels.

The man's real name was Gerd Keppler. He was the organizer and commander-in-chief of the Green and Black.

BY EIGHT IN THE MORNING, Keppler and his two companions were speeding downstream aboard a small, fast boat on the Ohio River. A stiff wind blowing against the current raised three-foot waves, bucking the speedboat and spraying the men on board.

Despite being soaked, Keppler was full of enthusi-
asm.

They didn't have far to go. A few miles down the
river they arrived at a heavily wooded island. It was
almost two miles long and a hundred yards wide, and
from the air looked something like a huge worm
crawling along the surface of the river.

"How can you be sure that it won't be discovered?" Keppler asked the man who had driven the
Mercedes.

"You'll see," the driver replied. The man's real
name was Oley and he'd been in the Ohio Valley
overseeing Keppler's interests there since the Green
and Black operation began. "She's thick with briars,
nettles and poison ivy. Muskeeters and jiggers, too,
like you wouldn't believe. Trust me, it's not the sort of
place that anybody would visit if they didn't have to."

In spite of all that, the Green and Black had estab-
lished a camp on the island.

Oley guided the speedboat to a camouflaged landing on the West Virginia side of the island. He bent
over the bow and tied the boat's mooring rope to a
ring under the water. In a moment the boat began to
shudder, and then it rose. The ring was at the front of
a submerged conveyor contraption that dragged the
speedboat along a pair of all-but-invisible steel tracks.
Within a minute, the boat had disappeared inside the
thick brush on the island.

What Oley had said was true. It was no wonder no
one came ashore. The island was uninhabitable. In
addition to the nastiest vegetation imaginable, mosquitoes swarmed in air that seemed as humid as that

of a tropical jungle. There were millions of gnats, probably black flies, and even though Keppler saw no snakes, there was no reason to doubt they were there.

A nearly naked man walked toward them, his body streaming sweat. He wore a sweatband above his eyebrows and sneakers on his feet. Besides his loincloth, these were the only clothing on his slender, muscular body.

"Keppler," he said calmly. "At last." The "at last" wasn't a phrase of welcome, really. It was sarcasm, clearly meant to convey the message that Keppler should have arrived here a lot earlier.

"Takahashi," Keppler said in a way of a greeting.

Sako Takahashi was the last effective survivor of the Red Swords, the Oriental terrorist cabal all but eliminated by the Executioner five years earlier. Since that time, Takahashi's reason for existence could be reduced to a common denominator—hate. Like most terrorists, he cared little about what he destroyed, as long as he destroyed.

By contrast, Keppler was an eminently practical man. Granted, he was also unhindered by morals when it came to matters of destruction. But his actions were born not out of blind hatred—an emotion he found inconvenient—but rather out of an insatiable lust for power and money.

Both men loathed their unlikely partnership, but agreed it was necessary.

Keppler moved in circles where Takahashi couldn't. Keppler could buy weapons with money from secret bank accounts. Takahashi could hardly walk through the door of a bank without setting off an alarm. On the other hand, the world's most vicious extremists rallied to Takahashi, recognizing him as a man of similar goals and strengths. The Japanese could supply troops. Keppler couldn't.

Each man was determined to kill the other as soon as this collaborative venture was over.

They walked along a narrow, twisting path into the interior of the island. How the scantily clad Takahashi could endure the place was more than Keppler could understand. He seemed to glide through tangles of thorns without being touched, and ignored it.

Camouflaged guards of varied racial and ethnic origin stared at them from their posts in the underbrush. The hard-faced men carried assault rifles and also seemed unperturbed by their surroundings.

About 150 yards into the brush they reached a camp that consisted of one large, screened-in tent surrounded by half a dozen smaller ones. Just beyond the camp, sweating men were engaged in heavy labor, carrying baskets of earth yoked over their shoulders.

The tunnel they were digging was more than that— it was a bunker, dug down and into the earth. Keppler could see a little distance into it. The walls and roof were lined with timber giving it the appearance of a mine shaft.

"Everything goes in there," Takahashi said. "Out of sight from the air, no matter what they use to spy on us. After everything is in, then even these tents will be removed from the island. No one will know we were ever here."

"Too much is committed to this place," Keppler stated. "It's bad strategy to—"

"That has been discussed and decided," Takahashi said briskly.

Keppler glanced around, disgusted with the squalid camp and the stench of the men digging the bunker. Other than two or three Orientals—Japanese, like Takahashi—the laborers were Middle Easterners. As far as Keppler was concerned, the compact men made suitable laborers—servile types who could dig holes—but little else. They were too conspicuous in this part of the country, and their misguided fanaticism represented a danger to his plans.

Keppler was there to oversee the realization of those plans—whether Takahashi liked it or not.

"Where is everything now?" Keppler asked.

"Some of it is already in the bunker. The rest is under traps around the woods. Within a few days, everything will be moved into the hole."

"Everything... You don't *have* everything."

"I believe that is *your* responsibility." Takahashi made no attempt to hide his venom.

"I came to see if you are ready."

"As you can see, I am."

"Then it will begin coming," Keppler told him. "Tons of it. Do you have room in there for *tons* of explosives?"

"Plus everything else," the Japanese replied.

"What about the dope?" Keppler pressed.

"We can always use more. We've built up quite a trade."

"I'll take whatever money you're holding beyond what you require to pay for your immediate needs."

Takahashi smirked. "I expected you'd want the money. I've got a little more than two million."

Keppler looked at him suspiciously for a moment, then let it go. If Takahashi was going to hand over two million, he'd taken in twice that. "We'll have to keep the trade going for a while. Two million won't be enough to pay all the bills. I'll get a new supply of junk in here in the next two or three days."

"Are you postponing the climax?" Takahashi asked suspiciously.

Keppler grinned. "My friend, we've opened a whole new market for narcotics. Apart from making enough money to pay the expenses of this operation, you and I have to make enough to make it worth our trouble." His grin broadened. "In fact, it's going so well, we might want to keep putting off the climax. Hell, man. We've got a winning business going here."

That was what Takahashi had been afraid of. Not that he had any problems of conscience with regard to dope dealing—he didn't. It was just that with an operation of this scale, there were already enough variables to be concerned about. On the other hand, weapons were expensive. So when Keppler first approached him, Takahashi reluctantly agreed, figuring that profits from the junk trade would easily finance other ventures, as well.

Takahashi glanced toward a group of the men carrying baskets of sand out of the bunker. "Don't let *them* hear any such talk," he warned. "They've got a different agenda. And they'd just as soon slit your throat as have you change it."

"Then, we won't let them know how much you've knocked off for yourself, either," Keppler said. "They think it's all going for weapons and explosives, for their cause. You and I have a dirty little secret, Sako. I'll keep mine. You keep yours."

IN THE DRIFTING MIST that so often shrouded the river at dawn, a small johnboat approached the West Virginia shore opposite Pomeroy, Ohio. The young man at the oars was named Leroy Gibbons. He was twenty-two years old and had lived on the river all his life. Rowing along the still water, he saw a big snapping turtle lying in the mud. He was tempted to go after it. Their meat was tasty, and he'd made many a dollar, in times gone by, catching turtles.

This morning, however, he had something better to do. In a plastic garbage bag on the floor of the boat lay a supply of white powder that would bring him more money than two hundred turtles.

Another man noticed the snapping turtle, and he, too, had chosen to ignore it. He sat on the trunk of a fallen cottonwood tree and watched Gibbons through a pair of binoculars, taking special notice of the green plastic bag.

His name was George Ellis. He was forty years old and had been a coal miner around southern Ohio and northwestern West Virginia all his life. He was a hard-working, God-fearing man who'd struggled to bring up his kids right.

Until recently, he thought he'd succeeded. His oldest son was produce manager in a big supermarket in

Parkersburg. His oldest daughter was married to a good-looking fellow who sold Dodge cars and trucks, and wore a necktie and a jacket to work. On the whole, they'd turned out all right. That is, except for Brenda. Only seventeen years old, she liked the poison Leroy Gibbons was bringing to shore. She liked it so well that she'd done things for it that had made him weep. After it made him weep, it had made him want to do something about the person who sold it to her.

The long tow that Gibbons had met was still in sight, two miles up the river. Ellis had watched him row out to one of its barges and make a deal for the plastic bag. Ellis didn't have to be told what was in it.

The damned thing was that the sheriff didn't seem to be able to do anything about it. Even if he'd known that Gibbons was bringing the stuff in, a man with two deputies couldn't watch the whole river twenty-four hours a day. Leroy was a river boy and could come in anywhere.

George Ellis sighed. He closed his eyes and asked the Lord's forgiveness for what he was about to do.

Then he picked up his Winchester lever-action .30-.30. Patiently he took aim at the middle of Gibbons's back and squeezed off a shot. The sharp crack of the rifle echoed across the river, and the youth jerked, then slumped forward on his seat, oars still gripped in his hands. To be sure, George Ellis levered another shell into the chamber and put another slug into the base of his neck.

Ellis put the rifle across his lap and thought of Brenda. He wasn't naive enough to think that nobody would take up the trade again. But maybe the next guy would understand it was dangerous to bring that stuff here.

3

The mission was moving along slow, too slow for the Executioner. After eliminating the drug runners on the previous night, Bolan was still no closer to the Green and Black than he had been before he'd arrived on the *Henry J. Muldoon*. In fact, he'd seen no evidence to connect the recent influx of narcotics in the Ohio valley to the terrorist group. Inaction didn't sit well with a man who was accustomed to being on the firing line.

Bolan had slept only a couple of hours before he was in the galley talking to Lisa, the cook. Known for her ability to memorize the names and faces of a crew instantly, Bolan hoped that she could be of some assistance. One of the crewmen had been on the barge to meet the drug runners the night before, and he'd gotten away. If that man was anything like Bolan suspected—a regular tow worker, trying to cash in on some fast money—the demise of his three suppliers would have shaken him up. Maybe he'd oversleep or give himself away in some other manner.

But as Bolan watched the men file past, many greeting him with the cold stares he'd now become accustomed to, he learned nothing. After a while, Lisa announced that everybody was accounted for, and a frustrated Mack Bolan returned to the pilothouse.

"We'll be going through a lock shortly," Captain Tolliver said. "You'll get an idea of the risks."

The risk lay in that the tow had to be taken apart. This lock, one of the older ones, wouldn't take fifteen barges and the *Henry J. Muldoon* all at once.

As they approached, the downstream doors of the lock opened. Tolliver maneuvered his barges into line and shoved them through the doors into the big lock chamber. The lock could take twelve barges—three wide and four long. Deckhands scrambled to lash the front barges to cleats on the lock walls, then to release the cables that bound the tow together.

With the *Muldoon* and its last three barges separated from the first twelve, Tolliver reversed the engines and backed the towboat and three barges out of the lock.

The downstream doors slowly closed. The lockmaster opened valves, and water from the pool above the dam began to gush into the lock chamber. The level of the water gradually rose, until the twelve barges stood ten feet or more above the towboat and the remaining barges. When the level of the water in the lock matched the level of the pool above the dam, the upper doors were opened. The process was repeated for the towboat and its three barges.

As the entire tow moved out of the lock and upstream, Tolliver nudged his vessel up to the twelve barges, and the deckhands hustled to reattach the thick cables and ratchet them tight.

"Those men earn their money," Tolliver said after the tricky procedure was completed. "If one of them fell overboard when we were still in the lock, you'd tell the family that he was washed away."

"Why's that?" Bolan queried.

"He'd be crushed an inch thick. You wouldn't want to let them see him."

"What if something else happened in the lock," Bolan asked, "like if a boat sank in there?"

"It'd block the river," Tolliver replied. "A boat sunk in the lock would stop traffic both ways, for however long it took to get it out of there."

"And if a downstream boat hit the doors the way *Grove City* hit the bridge at Marietta—"

"I don't even want to think about it."

HALF AN HOUR LATER, *Henry J. Muldoon* rumbled past the Muskrat Island where Takahashi and his men continued to dig their bunker. Bolan studied it casually, but saw no sign of the terrorist gang that had made their camp there.

Above Marietta, as the *Muldoon* passed by the ruins of the bridge, Bolan boarded an outboard-powered skiff that came alongside. He was taken into town, where he was met by the local sheriff.

To Sheriff Jack McGraw, Mack Bolan was Mike Belasko, a plainclothes officer of the West Virginia State Police. The state of West Virginia had provided the Sensitive Operations Group with the appropriate credentials, including a small gold badge in a leather case.

"We'll do anything we can for you, Sergeant Belasko," Sheriff McGraw stated, using the title of rank he'd read off the West Virginia ID card.

"Make it Mike."

"Okay, and I'm Jack. So what can we do for you?"

"I need anything you've got on who took over that towboat and rammed the bridge," Bolan replied. "You might know some things the Feds or the state police don't."

"I got some ideas," the sheriff said. "But right now I suggest we not be seen around together. It'd mark you as a lawman, and maybe you don't need to be known as one."

"You got a point."

"I'll drop you off at the car rental place. After you get your vehicle and check in at the hotel, pop in the office this afternoon, say two o'clock. I'll tell you my ideas."

ON McGRAW'S recommendation, Bolan took a room at the Lafayette Hotel. He followed the sheriff's suggestion that he spend some time in the hotel dining room, which would give him a picture of what kind of place Marietta was. He sat down in a booth, wearing a blue blazer, a white golf shirt and gray slacks. His Beretta 93-R rode in a shoulder holster, out of sight under the blazer.

The dining room was decorated to look like those of river steamers a century ago. It was obviously popular with the locals.

It was impossible for the warrior to be inconspicuous—people glanced at him, sizing him up.

One man stared thoughtfully at him for a long moment, then seemed to make a point of not turning his eyes in Bolan's direction again. The man didn't look like he belonged there. The cut of his clothes, his haircut, the solemn, studious look in his eyes clearly told Bolan that he wasn't a local.

Catching the waitress's attention, Bolan ordered a coffee and said, "I think I know the man at the table. Do you know who he is?"

"You might know him if you're from Texas. His name is Benjamin Johnson. They say he's come here to open a new oilfield."

SHERIFF JACK MCGRAW WAS a young man. Without the gray straw hat that was part of the prescribed summer uniform for Ohio sheriffs, his brown hair was fashionably long. He wasn't very tall, but he had a square, muscular frame. He carried a .357 Magnum Smith and Wesson revolver in a woven-leather holster.

"I don't think it's just a coincidence," he said, sitting in his office in the courthouse, "that the sudden plague of heroin and cocaine we've got in the Ohio Valley comes at the same time when guys in masks seize a tow and ram it into the I-77 bridge. I haven't got any way to chase down those guys in the masks. But I've got a drug dealer in custody, and I bet she—"

"She?"

The sheriff nodded. "From Marietta College. Her passport says her name's Jasmin al-Said, but everybody calls her Jazz."

"Passport from what country?" Bolan asked.

"Lebanon. There's a long-time connection between Marietta College and the American University of Beirut. Anyway, we caught her with 2.2 kilograms of cocaine. She's going away for a long time. She'll do ten years minimum before she's deported."

"She talk?" Bolan asked.

"Not to me, she won't. She figures I don't have the authority to help her out, which is right, I don't. But, supposed I was to introduce you to her as a narc?"

Bolan shrugged. "Why not?" Maybe the gunfight aboard the *Muldoon* wouldn't be a complete loss, after all.

"She hasn't had a visitor since she's been here, around two weeks now, so she's not likely to talk to anybody about the narc that came to see her."

The small-town jail had no cells for women, just a cage with four cots, a toilet and a shower. That afternoon the jail held two women, Jasmin al-Said and a fat, blowsy blonde whose face was scarred by gin blossoms.

"Hey, Jazz," McGraw called, "come here. I've got somebody to talk to you."

Jasmin al-Said rose from the cot and walked close to the bars of the cell. Even with her gloomy expression, she was an extraordinarily attractive girl. She wore a gray sweatshirt and blue jeans, and her head was covered with a white silk scarf wrapped loosely around her neck and shoulders. She had big brown eyes and an olive complexion.

"Sit down, Sally," the sheriff snapped at the drunken blonde. "This is none of your business."

The blonde sat down heavily, and Jasmin al-Said leaned against the bars.

"Mike Belasko," McGraw said quietly to the girl. "He's a narc and maybe a chance to do something for yourself."

It was as apparent that the girl didn't believe the sheriff—not that the big man wasn't a narc, but that he couldn't do anything for her. If Bolan could read faces, he read into this one that the girl had resigned herself to a deep and final personal tragedy.

What McGraw didn't understand was that "Mike Belasko" could, in fact, do something for the girl. Bolan didn't intend to lie to her. If she helped him in any important way, he could put a word in with Brognola. But most importantly, Bolan needed answers, and he needed them fast.

The sheriff backed away from the bars. "Talk to the guy, Jazz."

The girl looked at Bolan with eyes that were both defiant and sad, and she shook her head.

"It's up to you," the Executioner said. "You're looking at a lot of years in a place like this, followed by deportation. And you don't seem to have any friends. You have a lawyer?"

She shook her head.

"Well, you should have. If you did, I think he'd advise you to cooperate with me."

"What do you want?" she asked.

"Two kilos isn't a college girl's personal stash. I want to know where it came from and where it was going."

Jasmin al-Said shook her head. "I have nothing to say. Nothing." There was an almost imperceptible grin on her face that told Bolan plenty.

The warrior went back to the sheriff's office. They sat down, and McGraw swung his feet up onto his steel desk.

"Now *I've* got a suggestion for *you*," Bolan said.

"Glad to have one."

"Get her out of here. She's not planning on staying in jail. She's waiting for somebody to bust her out. Transfer her to a bigger town, where the jail is guarded by more men. Immediately."

"I'll see what I can do. It might take a couple of days."

"You might not have that long," Bolan warned.

BACK IN HIS ROOM at the hotel, Bolan found that it had been entered and searched.

They hadn't found anything. His weapons were locked in the trunk of his rented Chevy, as were several sets of fake ID. He'd expected a search on the *Henry J. Muldoon* and had taken the precaution of placing his weapons and ID in Captain Tolliver's safe. But it was strange to be searched so shortly after checking in at the Lafayette. The Executioner would very much have liked to know who was responsible.

Bolan left his room to check out the car. Finding it undisturbed, he took his things from it. He'd carry his papers and weapons in a battered leather case. Somebody's interest had been piqued, and that was a good sign. Things were starting to heat up.

The warrior didn't have time to scour the area in search of the intruder—who was probably long gone anyway—because he had someone else to see. Leaving the hotel, he drove up the river about fifteen miles and crossed a bridge into the village of St. Marys, West Virginia. There he went to the office of the sheriff of Pleasants County.

"Hello, Ed."

The Executioner and Sheriff Ed Higgins had worked together when terrorists had tried to poison the Ohio Valley by pouring a huge quantity of radioactive sludge into the river. Higgins remembered him well, although not as Mike Belasko.

"Nice to see you, friend. I must say, I never expected to see you back in this neck of the woods."

"No," Bolan replied, shaking his head. "I didn't, either. I'm back here because of the plague of narcotics you've got. And because of the bridge. I'd just as soon nobody knows anything about me."

"I saw you in action once, guy," Higgins said. "You can count on me."

"I know how the drugs are coming in. I'd like to get my hands on one of the dealers."

"Jack McGraw's got one locked up over in Marietta."

"Yeah, I saw her. She won't talk."

Higgins lighted a cigarette. He was an older man than Jack McGraw and a sadder man. Perhaps that was because he'd seen more. But Bolan remembered him as a brave man who wasn't afraid to use his gun. He knew he could count on him again for his help.

Higgins blew smoke and sighed. "I've never seen anything get people as worked up as this drug business. You know how it is. People in these little towns aren't used to it. And they're mad. Down in Mason County, a young fella that was bringing a load of cocaine ashore in a rowboat was just plain shot dead. I wouldn't be surprised if the sheriff down there knows who did it. I wouldn't want to be in his shoes and have to arrest the man that did it. In fact, I *wouldn't* do it—and I'll be surprised if the sheriff down there does it.''

''Can you help?''

''Well... How much time have you got? We could go out for a boat ride after dark. There's not much chance it'll do any good, but we might happen on something. As I remember, you've got your own way of taking care of things.''

SHERIFF JACK MCGRAW LEFT his office in the hands of two deputies, who alternated taking the overnight shift. One would sleep in a room adjacent to the office to be available to answer calls for help should they come. Most nights none did.

This night the man on duty was Gill Mayo. He was a sober man of forty-five and had served as deputy to the three sheriffs who preceded McGraw. A plodder and not quick to understand, he kept his job because he was totally reliable. It was a mistake to give Mayo too complicated an assignment, but given a simple job to do he labored at it until it was done.

A little before midnight the telephone rang. Mayo answered, and a minute later he was shaking Richardson, the other deputy, awake.

''Sam! You've got to get out to Whipple! Somebody held up the damn Busy Bee!''

Richardson rolled over on his cot. ''Hell of a lot of good it's gonna do to run out there. Whoever did it is in West Virginia by now.''

"Makes no difference. We gotta show up when something like this happens."

Sleepily Richardson rose from the cot and headed for the door.

Ten minutes later two men walked into the sheriff's office. They were dressed in black turtleneck sweaters and black pants, and wore black ski masks.

"Don't make trouble, and you may live to see tomorrow," one man calmly said. He had a silenced pistol in his hand that was aimed at Mayo's chest. "Now give, me the keys to the jail, my friend."

"You ain't gonna get 'em," Mayo replied. "I ain't gonna give 'em to you, and if you shoot me, you won't find 'em, 'cause you don't know where to look."

The two masked men exchanged glances. One of the men walked around the desk and he glanced around. It was true. The keys were nowhere in sight. He swung his pistol in a wide arc and smashed it into Mayo's jaw. The deputy slumped to the ground.

"We'll beat it out of you!"

For the next five minutes, they inflicted a savage beating, punching and kicking Gill Mayo around the face and belly. Bleeding, and barely conscious, he refused to tell them where to find the keys to the jail. Finally, with the deputy lying facedown in a pool of blood, one man took steady aim at the back of his head. His companion shook his head and shoved the muzzle aside.

"We got enough trouble without killing the old bastard."

4

Bolan was at first a little surprised at the boat, but he saw the wisdom of the sheriff's choice. Higgins had obtained a small johnboat with no motor, which meant they'd have to row.

The Executioner had dressed in the blacksuit and carried both the Beretta and the Desert Eagle. Sheriff Higgins had brought both a pump shotgun and a lever-action rifle in addition to two powerful flashlights, which wouldn't be used unless absolutely necessary.

They'd been on the river for more than two hours. To the Executioner, stakeouts came with the territory. Whether in the jungles of Vietnam or those of America's urban centers, the big man was an expert at it. The key was to be both focused and patient.

Unfortunately Sheriff Higgins had little experience with stakeouts and was getting restless. He passed the time by making conversation.

As they floated down the Ohio side of a big island just above St. Marys, two long tows passed each other. Higgins kept the johnboat close to the shore of the island to be well out of the way.

"We get some of the damned stuff," the sheriff continued, "but only a little. Our town has no great market for dope, but we're coming up to a good-size factory right downstream here. The folks that work there make money, and the poison's been showing up there. Apart from the barges this is as likely a place as any to run into something."

Floating along in the shadows of the shore, Bolan noted that a man got a different view of the river than he got from riding on a tow. The river was eerily quiet, and what little sound there was traveled a long way. Fish jumped occasionally, their splashes sounding far across the dark, still water.

"What's that?" Bolan asked, pointing to a brilliant light shining in a narrow circle just ahead of another johnboat at the foot of the island. A gasoline lantern burned inside a rude frame of wood and tin, directing the light straight down into the water.

Sheriff Higgins pulled on the oars and silently approached the johnboat.

There were two men. One sat on the bow, staring intently into the water. Poised in his right hand was a long pole with a three-pronged spear at the end. The other man stared at him. Neither saw the sheriff coming until his boat moved into their circle of light.

"Hi guys," Higgins called. "You wouldn't be out here gigging, would you?"

The man with the spear put it down across the boat and looked up, startled. "Reckon we are," he admitted.

Spearing fish under a bright light—or gigging as the river people called it—was illegal. A game warden would have issued a summons.

"Well, it's lucky for you that I'm looking for something else. I reckon you know what."

"It's not hard to figure out," said the man with the gig, more than a little relieved.

"Have you seen anything, then?"

"There's a couple of skiffs around Willer Island," the man replied. "It could be nothing, but they ain't fishin'."

The sheriff thanked the men and began to row. Going with the current, the johnboat moved briskly down the river. When they were far enough from the two fishermen to talk without being overheard he said, "Two skiffs, and the men aren't fishing. Now what else could they be doing? There isn't much to do besides fish on the river at this time of night."

From time to time the sheriff stopped rowing, and they sat and listened, Bolan's senses tuned to any sound that carried over the water. A light rain began to fall.

As the sheriff had said, a big manufacturing plant spread out along the West Virginia shore. Three big tanker barges were moored to a concrete wharf, which was lighted. The sheriff moved the boat so close to the Ohio side of the river that they had to duck under the limbs of trees along the shore. Out of sight from any boats on the river, they had a good vantage, because anything that floated would be silhouetted against the glow from the wharf.

Suddenly, no more than twenty yards ahead of them, a skiff moved out of the shadow of the riverbank and headed down the river. Bolan reached up and grabbed an overhanging limb to stop the johnboat.

Two men rowed the skiff, moving it as fast as they could. One of them spoke, but Bolan couldn't make out the words.

Higgins stood in the johnboat and pushed an oar into the river bottom to guide the little boat silently along the shore in pursuit.

The voice spoke again, and this time Bolan and the sheriff could hear the words.

"Yes or no?"

Another voice responded, but it sounded distorted.

"Where are you?"

It sounded like a radio, almost certainly a walkie-talkie.

"I'll show you one more time," the first voice replied. The skiff slowed, and Bolan could see a rope being thrown around the limb of a tree. Then the beam of a flashlight cut through the falling rain.

The sheriff began to say something, but Bolan put his finger up to his lips. It was obvious that they were waiting to meet another boat. And whatever their reason, they were being secretive.

Higgins shoved the blade of his oar into the mud and held the boat. They were close enough now that they could hear every word of the conversation.

"I hope we don't have to sit out here all night."

"For the kind of money we're makin', you'll damn well sit here all night—and half of tomorrow, too."

"Shut up, both of you!"

The third voice was sharp and had an accent Bolan couldn't immediately place. The johnboat was so close to the skiff that only the rain and the depth of the shadows prevented it from being seen.

A beam of light showed for a moment on an incoming boat. It was only fifty yards downstream, but rowing against the current was a slow process.

"Hurry up, dammit!"

"Well, you ain't been easy to find."

The incoming boat bumped against the waiting vessel. Bolan counted four men, two in each boat. While it was difficult to judge in the darkness, he had little doubt that they were armed.

"I'm not gonna weigh your stuff."

Then the sharp, accented voice said, "We don't have time, anyway. In this business, people who cheat die."

At that moment, Sheriff Higgins stumbled. Bolan grabbed the oar from his hand and shoved it hard into the mud, propelling the johnboat away from the shore.

"What the hell was that!"

A man in the rear of the second boat switched on a powerful flashlight and stabbed at the darkness with its penetrating beam. It caught the sheriff, who threw himself hard onto the bottom of the boat. The crack of a pistol followed instantly.

Bolan was quick to return fire, and a .44 slug punched the man with the flashlight backward into the river.

A shotgun boomed. The charge of heavy pellets ripped wood from the front of the johnboat and would almost certainly have hit them had Bolan not launched the boat downstream.

The warrior had counted on the gunmen shooting behind them and had already aimed at the point where he'd seen the muzzle-flash. He let loose three quick rounds, but couldn't see if he hit his target. There was banging and thumping in both skiffs as the drug runners threw themselves down in the hope of getting out of the way of the Executioner's deadly fire.

Bolan grabbed the other oar and used it to move the boat farther out on the river. Fire from the two skiffs tore into the water behind the johnboat as the current caught the vessel and carried it downstream.

Then automatic fire ripped through the night. The johnboat couldn't move quick enough as a spray of slugs tore through the tiny boat.

The Executioner fired at a muzzle-flash and saw the weapon jerk wildly up in the air as the man with the automatic rifle was knocked into the river.

The johnboat began to sink, but like any wooden boat, only partially. Kneeling, Bolan and the sheriff were up to their armpits in water. Although they'd lost what little maneuverability the johnboat had provided, sinking had in fact made them a smaller target. Slugs whipped over their heads as another automatic opened fire.

The sheriff emptied his revolver in the general direction of the two skiffs, which bought them a little time. The tiny johnboat had already drifted well past the two enemy vessels, and Bolan used an oar to paddle the sunken boat toward the shore. The men in the skiffs lost sight of them, and their firing stopped.

As the wreck of the johnboat neared the shore, the Executioner was already up the bank and racing toward the skiffs with the sheriff in tow.

The hardmen risked using their flashlights. After sweeping their beams over the water for a minute or so, they at last spotted the sunken johnboat drifting down the river.

"By God, we got 'em," one man said.

"Even if we did, we got big trouble. The Arab's dead, and I don't see the big guy that went down in the water."

"Thing to do is to get the hell out of here."

Bolan spoke from the bank above them. "The thing to do is to put your hands up and don't try—"

The shotgun boomed. The charge tore through the brush ten feet from either Bolan or Sheriff Higgins, who were both safely under cover behind trees.

The sheriff stepped out and aimed his service revolver with both hands. He fired four shots before Bolan could stop him.

Bolan held a flashlight far out to his right and risked switching it on. Higgins had taken out the last two. They lay in the bottom of their skiff.

The Executioner cursed silently. He needed one of the drug runners to give him answers. He scrambled down the bank, hoping to catch someone still alive.

The man they'd called "the Arab" lay in the shallow water beside the tied-up skiff. He was a Middle Easterner, maybe a Palestinian. As Bolan approached, the gaping hole in the man's chest made it apparent that he wouldn't be providing any information.

The two skiffs were moored to each other, with one tied to the tree. Two plastic garbage bags lay on the boat's floor under the corpse of the shotgunner. His companion lay draped—and equally dead—over the bow.

Bolan grabbed the plastic bags and tossed them overboard. Then he fired shots through each, sinking them and dissolving the poison they contained.

The skiff that had come from across the river was equipped with a powerful outboard motor and would be an able substitute to get them back to St. Marys.

As the sheriff sped the boat upriver, the Executioner reflected that a lot of little battles didn't necessarily win a war.

BOLAN RETURNED to the Lafayette Hotel as the sun was rising. He entered through a rear door and up the steps to his room, avoiding the deskman and anyone else who might see that he'd been out all night.

When he went down to the lobby a couple of hours later, the young woman at the desk had a message for him.

"Call Jack," it said simply. It had come in the night before at about 1:00 A.M. Bolan went to a telephone booth and called Sheriff Jack McGraw.

"You were right about one thing," McGraw said, sounding angry and more than a little tired. "Somebody tried to break Jasmin al-Said out of jail last night and in the process beat up my deputy pretty badly."

"Tried to break her out?"

"Yeah. My deputy's a faithful soul, and he wouldn't give them the keys. He's always kept them hidden just in case something like this happened. They worked him over hard, but she's still here, temporarily. I'm moving her to another jail as soon as I can."

"I'd like to talk to her one more time before you take her away."

"Be my guest."

Bolan arrived at the courthouse fifteen minutes later. Jasmin al-Said had been brought out from the jail and was sitting in the sheriff's office, heavily chained.

Jack McGraw took Bolan aside and talked to him out of her hearing.

"She doesn't know where she's going," he said. "The way I look at it, they can't try to break her out of another jail if they don't know where she is."

"Where *are* you taking her?" Bolan asked.

"Not far. Just to Cambridge."

"Tell the deputies who are taking her to drive on to Columbus and back," the warrior suggested. "We'll keep her friends guessing as well. I assume she knows why she's being moved."

"Sure she does. She heard them working over Gill."

"Let me talk to her again."

McGraw closed his office door, and Bolan sat behind his desk. Jasmin sat hunched forward on a plain wooden chair. She was handcuffed to a steel security chain around her waist, and her ankles were bound with leg irons. But vulnerable as she was, the girl's face was a mask of defiance.

Bolan stared at her for a long moment. His steely stare was no match for the prisoner, who dropped her gaze. "It didn't work and where you're going, they won't try again. You might as well talk."

"I want to go home," she said simply.

"Where's home?"

"Qatar," she replied.

"You have a Lebanese passport."

"I was attending the American University of Beirut, but my father decided it was too dangerous for me to remain there. So he paid the appropriate bribe and got me a Lebanese passport. It was the easiest way to get me a visa into the United States."

"Why Marietta?" he asked.

"My father's a wealthy and progressive man," she said. "He wanted me to get a good education, and Marietta is a good school."

"Why'd you get yourself involved in narcotics?"

She looked away from him for a moment, frowning. She started to lift her hands to make some kind of gesture but jerked against her chains and let her hands fall back in her lap.

"I can't expect you to understand," she said. Tears of sadness and frustration began to well in her eyes.

"You'd be surprised what I would understand." The Executioner uttered the words simply, not as a man looking for a confidant, but as a determined man who demanded the truth.

"I did it for the oppressed, particularly the Palestinian people. By playing on the depraved appetites of the Americans we were trying to raise the money to stage a major demonstration."

Bolan knew this sort of twisted logic well. Trade one sort of oppression for another. What sickened him most was the way the terrorists used it to prey on the misguided intentions of the young.

"What were you going to do with a kilo of the stuff? You couldn't have sold that much yourself."

She shook her head. "I never sold it. I only moved it. It came ashore from the boats and I simply passed it on. Who would suspect that the innocent princess was a courier?"

"'Princess'?"

She raised her chin. "My father, though not in power now, is an emir."

"Does your father know that you're in jail for dealing narcotics?" Bolan asked. He knew he hit a nerve. Jasmin shook her head as tears began to run down her cheeks.

"He *can't* know. Even when the people from the college came saying they'd retain a lawyer for me, would raise bail and all that, I knew he'd find out. I told them to go away and leave me to handle my own affairs."

"So they came and tried to rescue you last night. Well, they failed and now you'll be moved somewhere where you can't be rescued. Are you ready to ask for help?"

"I can't do anything that will allow word to get back to my father. It's better that he think I'm dead."

Bolan sat and stared at her, allowing her to think awhile.

"Suppose it could be arranged for you to go home and for everything that's happened to be kept secret," Bolan said.

"What do I have to do?" she asked.

"Tell me who supplied the cocaine, how they delivered it to you, where you took it and who picked it up from you. You might have to look at a lot of pictures."

"Where will I be?" she whispered. "In what prison?"

"Where they can't rescue you, and also where they can't come to kill you."

Jasmin sighed. "I know one name—Sako Takahashi."

IN A PUBLIC TELEPHONE booth on a street corner, Bolan punched in the confidential number that got him directly through to Hal Brognola.

"You wanted to trade intel," he said to Brognola. "I've got some, and I've also got an informer. But her name has to be kept absolutely quiet. She's a Qatari princess. She's in jail for possession of cocaine, and she's willing to talk. Two hardguys tried to break her out of jail last night, and they'll probably try to kill her if they guess she's talking. I want her protected."

"Where is she now?"

"She's still in the county jail here. They were going to move her, but I talked the sheriff into playing a little game. Another woman was chained up and taken out of town in a squad car. She kept a jacket over her face when they led her out. Jasmin al-Said was moved to a juvenile cell, so nobody else knows she's still here."

"I'll get right on it, Striker."

"Another thing, Hal. If you can do it, send a Muslim woman to look after her. The girl is a devout Sunni Muslim."

"She's worth all this?"

"She gave me a name," Bolan said grimly. "Sako Takahashi. She says he's here. She doesn't know where, but he's here."

"You mean your old buddy of the Red Swords?"

"The same," Bolan replied. "And you can figure Takahashi doesn't play any small-time games. He's connected to the drugs, and it's a sure thing that he's Green and Black. If he's here, we've got bigger trouble than we thought."

AHMED MALIK WASN'T THE first to wonder why Sako Takahashi wasn't affected by the tortures of Muskrat Island. In spite of heavy clothing and chemical repellents, every other man suffered from mosquitos, poison ivy, nettles and just about anything else that bit, burrowed or scratched. Malik couldn't ask him, as it would have been a personal question.

No one asked personal questions of Sako Takahashi. Or challenged his authority. Or failed him.

The two men who had been sent into Marietta to break out Jasmin al-Said hung by their ankles from the limbs of a big sycamore tree. Naked, bound and their mouths stuffed with rags, they moaned but had ceased to struggle. Takahashi would kill the men himself sooner or later.

He worked alongside his men most of the time, digging in the bunker, carrying out dirt and shoring it with timber. None of them worked harder than he did, and none of them ate or drank less. He was a truly menacing presence to the men around him.

Malik came to the island only when he had something important to report. He was busy enough overseeing the Green and Black's various other operations.

"They moved her," he reported. "They took her out of the jail this morning, put her in a car and drove off with her. I tried to follow, but they cut me off."

"Cut you off?" Takahashi asked coldly.

"They ran a red light, and a city police car moved into the intersection and blocked traffic. By the time I could get around him, the car carrying the girl was out of sight."

"Brilliant work," Takahashi sneered.

"I swear to you I couldn't get past the police car. They planned the way they blocked everybody."

"But you saw her?"

Malik nodded. "They had her in chains in the back seat of a car and—"

"How do you know they didn't drive around town and come back?"

"I thought of that. I went back to the courthouse and looked for the car. I'd taken the licence number, so I kept an eye on the courthouse garage for two hours. It didn't come back."

Takahashi paced around Malik slowly. The Arab kept perfectly still so as not to show his fear of what the Japanese would do. Takahashi played this game often and was known to pounce upon those who flinched. After an agonizing amount of time, he turned around to face Malik.

"I have another assignment for you, Malik. Keppler thinks the tall, dark-haired man who calls himself Belasko is somebody. He doesn't know who, he's just got an instinct about it. I want him eliminated as soon as possible. Tonight. I don't care how you do it. When he's dead, if you think you could be identified and arrested, come back here.''

Malik nodded gloomily. He knew that hiding here would mean working in this hellhole alongside Takahashi and his sweating crew of diggers.

"You understand? You can walk up to him in the hotel lobby and shoot him in sight of a dozen witnesses. I don't care. If you can get away with it and stay in the town, fine. If not, do it and come here.''

Malik nodded. He understood.

5

In Bolan's estimation, working the river had been considerably less than successful. There'd be a few less people to run the poison, but he had no illusions that they wouldn't quickly be replaced.

He also had no illusion that Sako Takahashi had become a cocaine peddler. The Japanese worked on a larger scale. Something bigger was coming down, and since Bolan was powerless to find Takahashi, he intended to dismantle his operation from the bottom on up. Cocaine might come ashore in various ways, but sooner or later it had to find a market. Tonight, the Executioner was going to find that market—in town.

Aware that nothing consequential would be achieved in broad daylight, Bolan took the precaution of checking into a second hotel outside of town in the name of Rance Pollock. He'd lived this long by avoiding making a target of himself. After bringing the leather suitcase up to his room, the warrior checked his weapons, then settled down to a couple of hours of sleep.

AHMED MALIK WAS SURPRISED. He had waited in the lobby for three hours, watching for the man called Belasko. His compact 9 mm Smith and Wesson hung by his left armpit, ready to be drawn. He'd sat sweating those three hours, hoping that Belasko wouldn't show up. The thought of opening fire in the hotel lobby and having to seek shelter on Muskrat Island was more than he could bear.

But the big man was nowhere to be seen. Was it possible that he'd slipped in unnoticed? Malik was beginning to believe that this Belasko fellow was exactly what Takahashi suspected—a smart and dangerous man.

It was thus with even more trepidation that Malik took the elevator up to the American's room. Belasko was still an uncertain threat; Takahashi wasn't. Once outside the room, Malik drew his automatic then rapped on the door.

No answer, and no sound at all from inside.

Malik knocked once more. When he got no response, he decided that his target had either carried off a deception, or flown the coop. Either way, he was in it deep.

Deciding it better to face the music now rather than later, Malik went to Keppler's room and knocked. The heavyset man opened the door and beckoned Malik in with a toss of his head.

"Well?"

"Belasko hasn't been in the hotel all day. He hasn't checked out, but he's not around."

Unlike his partner, Keppler concealed his anger behind a cold appraising gaze. Malik couldn't decide who was more unsettling.

"Go find him. Look for his car first. If it's in the hotel parking lot or on the street, then he's somewhere close. Look for him."

"And if that doesn't work?"

"Then work the town. It's looking more and more like I was correct about our big friend. Oley will come with you," Keppler said, nodding at the big, rawboned man. "He knows how to use a gun."

Oley stood. He was wearing a nylon jacket and reached inside to pull out an immense .357 Magnum revolver. "What do ya say we have some fun?" he said with a broad grin.

MARIETTA WAS A SMALL CITY in the image of a thousand others like it all over America. At the junction of the two rivers, it took advantage of its riverfront attractions. A hundred years ago the streets had been lined with shops, saloons and brothels. The riverfront had been the focus of Marietta's activity—shipping, commerce and vice.

Now, the city was trying to revive the romantic aura of those days. Gaslights cast a greenish glow over brick pavements. However, where men had once drank themselves into stupors at the bars of crude saloons, men and women now sat at the tables of tasteful cafés and restaurants.

Entering the scene, freshly shaved and showered, Bolan wore a blazer that covered his holstered Beretta. Walking the streets, he saw no sign of drug dealing.

He went into a few bars and nursed a beer in each. In the first two he saw only people drinking and generally having a good time. But outside of the third, Bolan watched a small blond girl approach a couple on the street. She couldn't have been a hooker, but she might have been peddling something. The man shook his head in a friendly sort of way, and he and his companion entered an upscale place called the Pelican Lounge.

Bolan watched the girl for a minute. Like Jasmin al-Said, she was college-aged and attractive. After a moment, a young man approached her. They seemed to know each other and talked for a while before walking into the Pelican Lounge. Bolan followed.

It seemed to be a popular place as all the bar stools were taken. It was filled with pink light and inoffensive music. A few people danced on a small square of polished floor. A hostess greeted him, led him to a booth and took his order.

Bolan kept an alert eye on what was going on. The young couple was dancing—innocent enough—and the warrior began to think he might have been wrong about the girl. Still, it couldn't hurt to make sure.

A few people had turned and looked curiously at him when he arrived. It was unusual, apparently, for a man to go to the club alone. Almost everyone in the place was part of a couple or a group. They looked up and stared again as another lone man entered.

When the hostess offered to seat him, the man seemed to tell her that he didn't mind standing at the bar. Sober and concentrated, he soon had a drink in his hand. After a while, he turned his back to the bar and solemnly watched the four couples dancing.

The music stopped. Two of the couples returned to their tables. The one Bolan had been watching stayed on the floor. Another couple broke up. The man went to a table, and the girl stood and looked round, obviously looking for another dance partner. Her eyes stopped on Bolan for an instant, but he didn't look up or give her any encouragement.

She turned to the man standing with his back to the bar, who, Bolan observed, shook his head. But when the girl laughed and grabbed his arm, the man reluctantly put down his drink and stepped out on the floor with her.

They made an odd couple. The girl was petite, but fullfigured and lively. She wore a tight minidress and her hair lay on her bare shoulders. The man was short and square, with solemn dark eyes and an olive complexion. He danced stiffly and didn't seem to enjoy it. When the music stopped, he bowed to the girl and retreated to the bar to get his drink.

Then she came to Bolan.

"Come on, big guy," she coaxed. "One dance."

"I'm not good at it."

"If I didn't dance with guys who claim they can't dance, I'd never get to dance," she replied. "Come on."

Bolan grinned and moved out on the floor with her.

"Let's see," she said playfully. "You're an FBI agent, in town to investigate the bridge thing."

Bolan smiled. "I wish it was something as exciting. Actually I buy coal leases for a mining company."

"Sure you do!" she laughed.

They said nothing more until the dance was over. She didn't suggest he buy her a drink. Instead she went up to the bar and bought one for herself. Bolan was more than a little relieved to resume surveillance of the bar from his booth.

But before too long, the short, dark man from the bar came around the edge of the dance floor and approached Bolan.

"Am I in error in believing you and I have met?" he asked.

"I don't recall it," Bolan replied.

"Ah. Perhaps I *am* in error, but would you object to my sitting with you for a few minutes? I should rather not be prevailed upon to dance again."

Bolan grinned and pointed to the other side of the booth. The man sat down.

"I'm Ahmed Malik," he said quietly.

"Mike Belasko."

Malik fixed his eyes on the Executioner, as if he were trying to read something in the face of the bigger man. Bolan knew instantly that this man hadn't sat down with him by pure chance. He wanted something.

"Can I buy you a drink?" Malik asked.

"Thanks, but I'll stop with one," Bolan said. "It's a double."

"I, too, find the drinks here strong. So, if you'll forgive me—" Malik rose "—I will bid you adieu."

Bolan nodded as Malik turned to leave.

Just as Bolan began to ponder the encounter with the strange man, the girl he'd been dancing with slipped into the booth and sat down. "Is that guy a friend of yours?" she asked.

Bolan shook his head. "No friend of mine. I never met him before tonight."

"He asked who you were," she said. "Of course I didn't know either. But let me tell you something about the guy. He's carrying a gun."

Bolan had suspected as much and managed to sound casual as he asked, "How do you know?"

"I danced with him," she said simply.

"Well, thanks."

The girl grinned. "Between you two guys, I pick you." Then she left.

Bolan signaled the waitress to pay for his drink. It took too long, but after a while, he was on his way out the door. Maybe there'd been drug activity at the Pelican, but right now there were more interesting developments that demanded the Executioner's attention.

Outside, Bolan found himself at the end of a block of shops where the streets were dimly lighted. He walked cautiously toward the Lafayette hotel, which was closer to the river.

"*Psst!* Hey!"

Bolan swung around. The girl was standing in the shadows in a doorway. His expression told her that she wasn't the person he'd hoped to see.

"I'm not trying to pick you up, stupid," she said in a harsh whisper. "Check the blue Ford in the parking lot by the hotel."

He looked across the street. There *was* a blue Ford in the first rank of cars in the parking lot.

"Your friend with the pistol is in that car," she said. "The name's Donna Dow, and I've got no interest in whatever's coming down, man. No interest at all."

"Thanks," he said. "You better go back inside now."

She nodded and raised her chin. "Sure thing, coal buyer. Good luck."

Bolan stepped away from her and walked between two parked cars into the street.

The driver's-side door of the blue Ford opened. Ahmed Malik slipped out and crouched behind it, taking aim with an automatic. In one quick motion, Bolan dropped to a crouch and drew his Beretta.

Malik didn't fire. He adjusted his aim and seemed to hesitate.

"Look out!" Donna screamed.

Bolan snapped around just in time to see a big man setting himself and taking aim with a big revolver.

The warrior threw himself to the pavement. The revolver roared, and its heavy slug gouged a hole in the ground exactly where he'd been an instant before.

Bolan rolled, and he jumped up with the Beretta aimed at the chest of the big man. The unsuppressed pistol cracked angrily.

The West Virginian didn't get a second shot. Oley dropped his revolver, and sank to his knees with a hole in his chest.

Bolan was already moving as Malik fired. He was no marksman, and his three shots cracked through the window of a store behind the warrior.

The Executioner's second shot hit Malik squarely at the bridge of his nose, the bullet boring through his brain and exploding out the back of his head.

Donna screamed.

Bolan ran to her. "Come on," he said. "I owe you. Let me get you out of here before the cops come."

Terrified, she backed away from him, deeper into the doorway.

"Let's go!" he urged. "You don't want to hear the questions that are going to be asked. You don't know the answers."

"What am I getting myself into?" she managed to whisper.

"Nothing. I'll take you home."

FROM HIS fourth-floor room in the Lafayette hotel, Keppler had watched the Executioner survive the attempt on his life by Malik and Oley, had watched him shoot down both of them. He also watched as Bolan led a blond girl away from the scene with his arm around her.

The city police arrived with two ambulances. Their red lights flashed, and the crowd poured out of the bars along the street. It had been a long time since the town had seen anything like this—if ever.

Kurt Steiner—the man checked into the hotel as "Frank Gunther"—stood behind Keppler, also watching. A former member of the Baader-Meinhof gang, he was a professional terrorist, and had been the other German's personal bodyguard for many years. Keppler wasn't sorry that he hadn't dispatched Steiner in place of Oley. The man was far too valuable to risk before knowing what he was up against. Besides, his heavy accent drew too much attention.

"So," Keppler said, "it is as we suspected. Our Mr. Belasko is a professional, very likely a counterterrorist agent for the U.S. government."

"That means we've killed two birds with one stone," Steiner said. "We're rid of Malik, and we've learned what we wanted to know."

"We send no more amateurs after Mr. Belasko, or whatever his name is."

"I'll take him out," Steiner said coldly.

"The girl in the minidress..." Keppler mused. "I wonder if it was a coincidence that she warned Belasko—or does she work with him? Either way, to get him we go after her. He won't let anything bad happen to his little heroine."

"I FIGURED IT WAS YOU," Sheriff Jack McGraw said. "Man, the shit's really hit the fan since you turned up. I got two men shot down in the street, and bodies in the river, one literally blown apart. A skiff loaded with plastic bags that had contained cocaine was shot full of holes, hit with a big gun, bigger than a .357 Magnum, I'd guess. Another one had ordinary .38 slugs in it. If we're going to work together, who—"

"Ed Higgins," Bolan told him. He'd been in the sheriff's office filling him in on recent events. But he also had some questions of his own.

"Anybody show up from Washington?"

"Damn right. Justice Department guys, plus a Muslim woman. They took Jazz. Do you know where?"

Bolan shook his head.

"Their credentials were good. I couldn't—"

"They were real," Bolan said. "Jasmin al-Said could get to be a diplomatic problem."

"Hey, you know… They took her fingerprint card. Mug shots. All the papers. So far as records are concerned, she was never here."

"I want to ask you about another young woman. What do you know about Donna Dow?"

"Donna…" The sheriff grinned. "Cute, isn't she?"

"She saved my life last night. Yelled out a warning about the guy behind me. If anybody knows that she warned me… You get what I mean?"

McGraw nodded. "What you want me to do?"

"Tell me about her, to start with."

The sheriff shrugged. "Cute girl. Her mother died years ago, and her father's a drunk. She lives in a room in an old lady's house and does some housework for her rent. She also works behind the counter at one of the local bowling alleys. Likes a good time. She married once, when she was eighteen, but is divorced now. No kids. Nice girl, really."

"I don't want anything bad to happen to her," Bolan said. "I'll notify the Justice Department, but in the meantime…"

McGraw nodded. "Let me make a call."

He punched in a number and waited for an answer.

"Hello, Charlie? Jack McGraw. I've gotta ask you for a favor, but strictly between you and me. I mean, strictly. You know that shootup on Front Street last night? Well, it seems Donna was a witness. Don't tell her this, but there's reason to believe that some guys might want to silence her. So I gotta ask you to let her off the job for a few days. Don't say anything to her. I'll be around to pick her up in ten minutes or so. Don't worry, I'm going to put her somewhere safe. Thanks, Charlie."

McGraw put down the phone. "You coming with me?"

Bolan nodded.

Two minutes later they were in the sheriff's cruiser on their way to the bowling alley.

BEHIND THE SNACK BAR of the Marietta Lanes, Donna Dow wiped her hands with a kitchen towel. She'd just changed into a pair of cutoff shorts and a tight black T-shirt. On the other side of the counter, Charlie Gleason, the owner of the bowling alley, stood beside two serious-looking men.

"I still don't see why I have to go with these guys," Donna said. "I've got no beef with anybody."

"That may be so. All the same, I just got off the phone with the sheriff and he said they'd be coming for you."

Donna eyed the men suspiciously. The one who'd done all the talking and shown ID was a brawny man with short-cropped hair and an ill-fitting suit. The other had sharp, chiseled features and wore his black hair slicked back. He hadn't said a word since they entered.

"How do I know you guys are with the sheriff?" she asked. "You don't even look like cops."

"As you know, ma'am," the brawny man began, "there's been a lot of crime around here lately. We don't want to be here any more than you. But the fact is, we're here for your protection.''

With that, Donna shrugged and walked out from behind the counter. "Well, we'd better go then.''

The silent man took Donna's arm and with his partner—Kurt Steiner—escorted her toward the exit.

BOLAN KNEW IT WAS BAD as soon as the sheriff's black-and-white pulled into the bowling alley's parking lot. Two men were shoving a woman toward a nondescript gray sedan parked far to the back of the lot. Although he was too far away to be positive, he had little doubt who the woman was. Bolan pointed a finger toward the scene.

"Shit!" the sheriff barked.

McGraw whipped the cruiser into a spot out of sight of the struggle, and the two men flung themselves out of the vehicle. The Executioner had already drawn his Beretta, as did the sheriff with his service revolver.

"Stick close to me,'' Bolan instructed. "We've got to get closer.''

Donna Dow was beginning to really put up a fight. Bolan and the sheriff were sidling along a row of parked cars when they saw the man with the slicked-back hair strike her.

Bolan recognized him instantly, and it sent a chill down his spine.

"Jack,'' he whispered, "I know that guy. He's dangerous. You take the other one and let me handle him.''

"You got it,'' McGraw said. "And you shoot first.''

The problem was, he *couldn't* shoot. Although Bolan was almost in range, Steiner held Donna close.

"Get the shotgun out of the car," Bolan muttered.

McGraw slunk back to the vehicle and extracted the short-barreled 12-gauge from its locked bracket.

When the sheriff returned, he took aim on the second man. Neither he nor Bolan had been spotted by Donna Dow's abductors.

McGraw checked with Bolan, who nodded.

When the 12-gauge roared, Steiner's confederate was swept off his feet by a flurry of buckshot that cut him almost in two at the belly.

Bolan was ready for Steiner's reaction. The German snapped his head toward his partner and in an instant reached for his pistol. In so doing, he threw Donna aside.

The Executioner didn't hesitate. He fired instantly.

But Steiner, too, was a fighter. He hurled himself to the pavement and scrambled into the shelter of two parked cars.

Bolan was confident that he'd hit the German. He stood and gestured for Donna to lie flat on the blacktop.

Terrified, she did as she was told.

The warrior slipped around the rear of a Buick and worked his way toward Steiner, just as McGraw fired two shots from the shotgun. They were useless except to let Steiner know the Executioner wasn't his only threat.

Donna crawled toward a car, meaning to slide under it. A slug punched through the rear fender of that vehicle and she stopped. Steiner had aimed, not to kill Donna, but to frighten her.

The German was smart. The warrior's slug had grazed his side, tearing away flesh and cracking a rib. Despite the pain, he understood that his adversary wanted to save the girl. He wouldn't kill Donna, because if he did, the two men would move against him without hesitation.

Bolan knew what Steiner was thinking. Once more Donna tried to crawl under the car, and again Steiner spanged a slug off the blacktop near her.

The Executioner had his position now, and he fired two shots through the window of the car where he knew Steiner was hiding.

McGraw, with a reloaded shotgun, hurried to follow the warrior's lead.

"Damn!" They both saw Steiner hobble up a hill twenty yards above the rear of the bowling alley and into a tangle of brush. McGraw let two shotgun blasts go, but they were nowhere near the mark. Bolan had already lowered his weapon.

"He's hit," Bolan said, "but he's also a marksman. If we run up into the woods after him, it'd be suicide."

The Executioner walked across the parking lot to the car where Donna Dow lay whimpering on the blacktop.

"Come out," he said gently. "It's over. You're safe now."

6

Mack Bolan left Donna Dow in the second hotel room he'd rented outside of town. Despite her protests that she shouldn't be left alone, Donna was calmer than she'd been when Bolan slipped her in a couple of hours earlier. And, in truth, she wasn't alone. Bolan had arranged for Jack McGraw to put a deputy in the room across the hall, with his door open. Nobody had seen them enter the hotel, so she'd be safe.

That left Bolan free to check on the three federal agents who were guarding Jasmin al-Said in a motel just outside Parkersburg, West Virginia. As he'd suggested, one of the agents was a Muslim woman who understood the girl's ideas about propriety and privacy. Jasmin still wore a sweatshirt and faded blue jeans, but her head was modestly covered with a white silk scarf. She also wore a pair of leg irons connected by a chain that was long enough to let her walk around the room without difficulty, but short enough to prevent her from making a dash for the door. Technically she was a prisoner being held on serious charges.

One of the agents was named Farrell. He handed Bolan a big yellow envelope that contained photographs wired to the Parkersburg police department from FBI headquarters. Bolan pulled one out and showed it to Jasmin.

"Who's that?" he asked.

"Takahashi."

Next, he showed her a picture of Kurt Steiner, but she didn't recognize the German terrorist and shook her head.

Finally he handed her a picture of Ahmed Malik.

"This man I know," she said. "I don't know his name."

That told the Executioner that Takahashi had sent Malik, but it still didn't account for Steiner's presence.

Bolan left the pictures with Farrell. "This one's dead," he told him, nodding at the photo of Malik. "The other two are a couple of the most dangerous men I've ever come across, and they're somewhere within twenty miles of here. Stay alert."

DOUG BROOKOVER SHOVED his cap back off his forehead and ran his hand across it, wiping away sweat. He took a last drag on his cigarette and flipped it away into the damp woods to the side of the road.

Even though it didn't make any difference, he never smoked around the stuff. As an expert, he knew perfectly well that fire wouldn't set off the kind of explosives stored in the sheds. Everything was set off by electricity, and the caps were inside sealed packages. Even so, to Brookover it seemed foolish to puff on a smoke when he was handling this kind of stuff.

The mining company kept its supply of explosives in a cluster of corrugated-steel sheds in a valley in the woods. They built their magazines in remote, steep-sided valleys, so if a big explosion occurred, the force of the blast could be contained. He'd seen a picture of a valley where nitro had gone off a hundred years ago. Perhaps that was why he was extra cautious.

Driving a Range Rover that the company provided, he was going to pick up three cases of dynamite, plus a carton of blasting caps. It was a rugged vehicle, perfect for the mud-slicked, bumpy roads that he'd been driving on. The power and handling gave Brookover confidence.

As he approached the storage depot, he noticed that someone had left the gate open. He'd raise hell about that when he got to the magazine. But as he rounded the last turn in the road, he saw two trucks that definitely weren't supposed to be there.

In another second the whole thing was clear. He jammed the Range Rover in reverse and threw up a cloud of dust trying to back out of the depot.

He wasn't quick enough. Bullets began punching through the windshield. He screamed in pain when a slug tore his left ear off. But the pain didn't last long. The next two slugs burst his skull.

"THIS HAS GOT TO HAVE something to do with something," Jack McGraw said to Bolan. "Forty cases of dynamite, two hundred pounds of gelatin and caps. They cleaned out the place."

"Was anyone killed?"

"The guard and a blasting guy who'd come to get his dynamite. The slugs they dug out of the blaster's Range Rover were 7.62 mm. That kind of ammo doesn't come out of somebody's hunting rifle. Anyway, who'd want forty cases of dynamite?''

"We *know* who'd want forty cases," Bolan said grimly. "The question is, where'd they take it?"

"Considering what we're afraid of, how about the nearest lock and dam?"

That's exactly what Bolan was afraid of. In his mind, he'd gone over how the Green and Black would try to fulfill their threat, but he'd come up blank. "The charge can't be set into the walls, like in drilled holes," Bolan said. "So, if they're going to try to take out a lock, they'll have to bring the dynamite in on a boat. That means our forty cases of dynamite are out on the river. But where?"

"If they went straight for the river, the nearest lock and dam is Racine. Of course, they could go downstream and hit the Gallipolis dam."

"Or they could go through one or two locks and look for one that's especially vulnerable," Bolan stated.

"The only place to find out is on the river."

THE NAME OF THE TOWBOAT WAS *Sterling Bradbury*. It was a working vessel, but of a different kind. The *Bradbury* didn't pick up strings of barges here and there. Its two barges stayed with it always, following the dredge boats that scooped up tons of sand and gravel from the river bottom. Then it carried those tons of sand and gravel to where they could be sold.

Today, the *Sterling Bradbury* was carrying out a special contract. The captain, Sterling Bradbury, Jr., was the only member of the regular crew aboard. He'd agreed to be locked in his cabin while his barges were loaded, and to also be locked in when they were unloaded. For this, he was receiving more money than he could make in a month on the river. He'd guessed—but didn't really want to know—what was under a shallow cover of sand in his barges.

"All I ask of you gentlemen," he said, "is that you don't bust up my boat. Besides that, you can haul the Devil himself on my barges for the money you're paying."

Standing beside him in the tiny, shabby pilothouse was a Syrian by the name of Najati Zuabi. He had made all the arrangements and paid in cash. So far the riverboat captain had been no problem. When the job was finished, it would be Zuabi's judgment whether to kill the boatman.

They had no intention of detonating the dynamite and gelatin in a lock, because there wasn't nearly enough to do what the Green and Black's leaders intended to do. The stolen explosives were on their way to the arsenal Takahashi was building on Muskrat Island. When the time came, it would be loaded aboard a big tow and set off with a blast that would astound the world.

BY THE TIME they reached their boat at Gallipolis, the sun had already begun to set. Bolan would have preferred a more powerful vessel, but their skiff had an outboard motor that would produce twice the speed as the tows—and it was inconspicuous.

In addition to Bolan and Sheriff McGraw, who kept a keen eye on the river, Deputy Gill Mayo was at the helm.

"You need a man to steer," he'd argued. "And nobody's going to stop me from getting back at them bastards."

Mayo hadn't shaved since he was worked over in the office, and his face bristled with white stubble. His head was swathed in thick bandages, but he was spry and alert.

McGraw had shrugged and said to Bolan, "How can I refuse a man who—"

"You can't."

Mayo turned out to be an unexpected asset, because he seemed to have an instinct for the river. He knew the currents and steered the skiff like a fisherman. He also had an eye for the towboats, and how to judge them.

Bolan and McGraw had briefed him about what was going on and what they were looking for.

"That boat over there," Mayo said, nodding toward a tow moving downstream. "That's the *Hardy*. It's Captain Livengood's and there's no way anybody's puttin' anythin' that he don't know about on one of his barges."

"What kind of boat are we looking for?" the sheriff asked.

"To what you're talkin' about," Mayo replied, "you'd have to take over a big tow. That'd take a lot of men, a lot of guns, and if you didn't do it right, the captain would be able to get off a radio call."

"You can't carry forty cases of dynamite in a skiff?" Bolan asked.

"Or get a lock to open for you, either. But that one going through the lock," Mayo said, pointing farther downriver. "He's carryin' a crew of three or four men, at most. No radio, likely. With a sand and gravel boat, shovin' two barges like that one, you could put all your dynamite in one of them and cover it up with sand."

The boat Gill Mayo was pointing at was the *Sterling Bradbury*.

Bolan studied the little towboat and its two rusty barges. The *Sterling Bradbury* had none of the comforts of a boat like the *Henry J. Muldoon*—no elaborate galley, no air-conditioned cabins, no crew lounge with television. It just churned up and down the river, burning diesel oil and delivering the sand and gravel that stood in three cone-shaped heaps.

"Tell me about the captain," Bolan said.

"Sterling works his butt off to keep her afloat," Mayo answered. "It was his daddy's boat and carried a lot of bootleg liquor back in Prohibition."

"How do we find out what's on it now?" Bolan asked.

"An Ohio sheriff's got no jurisdiction over that boat," McGraw stated. "But of course, we could try to scare them a little."

"If we put on our sheriffs' hats," Mayo said, "they ain't gonna know if we're Ohio sheriffs or West Virginian. If they don't have anything to hide, they'll just let us come aboard and look around. If they do—"

"It'll get a little tough," Bolan finished for him.

Their weapons were probably as good as they would need. Bolan had the Desert Eagle holstered on his right hip. The sheriff and his deputy had U.S. Army .45s. Out of the gun case in the sheriff's office they'd brought two M-14s and a short-barreled, Winchester 12-gauge shotgun. Their arsenal was old-fashioned, but effective. What concerned the Executioner was the vulnerability of the open skiff.

"This is above and beyond for you guys," Bolan said. "I can put you ashore and—"

"Forget that," Gill Mayo grunted.

Bolan looked at McGraw.

"Let's go," the young sheriff said.

The sheriff and his deputy jammed their hats on their heads, and Mayo gunned the outboard. In a moment they drew up beside the *Sterling Bradbury*, about ten yards away.

"Sheriff!" McGraw yelled through cupped hands. *"Coming aboard for a look-see!"*

Bradbury was at the wheel of his boat. He turned and looked at Najati Zuabi, who sat on the bench behind the pilot. Zuabi stood and peered down at the small skiff. It was difficult to make out anything in the fading red light of the sunset.

"What does he expect you to do?" Zuabi asked.

Bradbury shook his head. "Nothing, I guess. Just to come aboard and look around."

Zuabi stared thoughtfully at the skiff for a long moment. "Tell me," he said to Bradbury. "How often does the sheriff demand to come aboard and search your boat?"

Bradbury's brow began to bead with sweat. "Actually, never," he said. "When my daddy ran the boat, he—"

Zuabi raised a hand to cut off the captain. He paced around the little pilothouse for what seemed like an eternity to Bradbury, pondering his options.

"Sheriff! Coming aboard!" McGraw called again.

Bolan's combat instincts told him there'd be trouble almost immediately. Reaching for one of the M-14s, he spread himself as flat as the skiff would allow and motioned for the others to do the same.

Zuabi had made his decision. He reached back to the bench and picked up his weapon. It was a Chinese copy of the Soviet RPK—a 7.62 mm automatic rifle with a 75-round drum magazine, a heavy wooden stock and a bipod near the muzzle. Although the bipod was extended, Zuabi held the weapon to his shoulder and aimed it like a rifle.

His prolonged burst chopped the water near the rear of the skiff, then rose and cut through Gill Mayo's legs and through the outboard motor.

"No!" Bradbury screamed.

Just as the Syrian leveled the RPK for another burst, Bradbury leaped away from his wheel and threw himself on Zuabi, wrestling him to the floor of the pilothouse. But the Syrian was a younger man and knew how to handle himself. He drove a fist into the riverman's face, and Bradbury rolled back, bloodied and subdued.

Zuabi leveled the RPK at the captain's belly. "If I didn't need you to take the boat through the lock, I'd cut you in two right now," he growled.

Those were Najati Zuadi's last words. As he stood and turned the muzzle of the RPK toward the river once again, a short burst from the M-14 in the hands of the Executioner tore through his throat and severed his spine.

Mayo writhed in the bottom of the skiff. One leg was torn apart, spurting blood.

"Help him!" Bolan yelled at McGraw.

The damaged motor stopped, and the skiff quickly lost ground to the steadily churning towboat.

Zuabi hadn't been the only gunman aboard the *Sterling Bradbury* and the Executioner knew it. Another man stepped out of the engine room, taking a brief moment to find his target before taking aim with another RPK. It was a moment he didn't have. Mack Bolan was a marksman with the M-14, and he took out the gunner with a head shot before the man could raise the muzzle.

McGraw knelt over Mayo. With a pocketknife he began cutting strips from his own shirt to make a tourniquet. But Mayo wouldn't stay still. Unbelievably, though his hands trembled, Gill Mayo drew the .45 from his holster and began to fire shots at the towboat.

Bolan couldn't guess how many more men were aboard the towboat. He wasn't sure, either, if some of them were ordinary crewmen. With Mayo in agony from the pain of his wounds, he could easily have hit an innocent.

"Get that gun out of his hand," he barked at McGraw.

Just then, another burst erupted from a window in the main cabin. Slugs splintered the gunwales of the skiff just ahead of the sheriff and behind Bolan. Before McGraw could disarm Mayo, the deputy had seen where the shot had come from and fired a round into the cabin. He was way off mark, but he helped Bolan find his target. The warrior fired a quick burst that silenced the gunner.

By this time, the *Sterling Bradbury* had moved well ahead of the skiff. With nobody at the wheel, it had begun to veer toward the river bank. The skiff began to bob in the *Bradbury*'s wake.

A man carrying a rifle ran up the steps toward the pilothouse. It took Bolan an extra split second to steady his aim before he could squeeze off another burst. The rifleman threw up his arms and fell back to the deck.

The *Bradbury*'s lead barge plowed into the muddy bank with a slow crunch. With the full force of the towboat's big diesel still shoving it, the barge nosed up the bank, spilling sand and exposing the cases of explosives hidden beneath.

"Fix them sons of bitches," Mayo muttered.

"*No!*" Bolan yelled as he threw himself into the bottom of the skiff.

The sand and water muffled a bit of the explosion, but the blast lighted the evening sky. It tore the pilothouse from the towboat and threw it into the water. Most of the main cabin was thrown overboard, as well. The steel barge was ripped open and sank immediately, pulling the second barge down just enough that water poured in and it sank, too.

The cases of dynamite and gelatin that had been dispersed among the piles of sand in both barges bobbed up and were carried downstream on the current.

In the first instant of the blast, debris flew over the skiff like confetti—wood and glass, mostly, but also shreds of corrugated steel, hurled at high velocity and deadly to anyone it hit. Bolan was down, and nothing hit him. But Sheriff McGraw was on his knees working on Gill Mayo and was struck in the back by a chunk of two by four that knocked him down. It didn't seriously injure him. Mayo, being behind and under McGraw, wasn't hit.

When Bolan rose to his knees and looked at the wreckage of the *Sterling Bradbury*, he saw the sinking barges carrying the little towboat down by the tow cables. The towboat's engine went under and blew up when hot steel submerged in cold water.

"Dammit, Gill," McGraw muttered.

Mayo took one final look at the sinking hulk, then fainted from shock and loss of blood.

THEY WERE HAULED OUT of the water by West Virginia deputies and state police officers. Gill Mayo was rushed to a hospital.

McGraw identified himself as the sheriff of Washington County, Ohio, then identified Bolan as Mike Belasko of the West Virginia State Police—which he thought was the case. That created some problems because nobody recognized the big man, but two hours later, calls to and from Washington straightened that out. McGraw was allowed to continue thinking that "Belasko" was a plainclothes detective of the West Virginia State Police.

During the night doctors amputated Gill Mayo's right leg.

Back in Marietta at three in the morning, Bolan found Donna asleep in his bed in the hotel room. He'd entirely forgotten about her. He lay down quietly beside her, fully dressed, and went to sleep without waking her.

7

Donna Dow awoke and rolled out of bed without waking the big man beside her. She called room service and guessed what kind of breakfast he'd want. A porter wheeled it in and the smell of the coffee roused the warrior from sleep.

"Some kind of man you are," Donna chided. "Spent the night in bed with me and never woke me up."

"Spent about four hours in bed with you," he said, looking at his watch.

"Three," she corrected. "I've been up for a while. Really, how long have I got to hang out with you?"

"You won't be with me much longer. I'm taking you somewhere else."

"I could go and stay with my aunt in Coolville," she said.

"There are guys who want to kill you who would find you in Coolville. Look, this won't last long. A few days."

"Well, where is it you plan on taking me?" she asked.

"Not far. A place where three federal agents are on guard twenty-four hours a day."

FRESH AND FULL, Bolan and Dow were out of the hotel room within half an hour.

The warrior rapped firmly on the door of the motel
room where the Muslim woman and the two other
agents were keeping Jasmin al-Said. When he got no
answer, he used a thin blade to open the lock.

No one was in the room, and no one had checked
out. A small traveling bag lay open on a luggage stand,
and a book someone had been reading lay on the
nightstand by the bed.

Donna gasped. "Look!" She pointed in horror at
a dark bloodstain on the carpet near the bathroom
door.

They left the room, and Bolan locked the door. He
went to a telephone booth in a small shopping center
down the road and called the West Virginia State Police, identifying himself as Belasko. The sergeant knew
who he was—that is, knew that a guy named Belasko
had some kind of connection with the Department of
Justice in Washington and was to be given coopera-
tion. Bolan told the sergeant what he'd seen in the
motel room.

"Was one of those Feds a guy named Farrell?"

"Right."

"He's dead," the sergeant said. "Found in a Chevy
out on Route 2. Bullet in his head."

"He was guarding a witness, and she's missing,"
Bolan told him. "An arab girl, young, good-looking.
She keeps her head covered with a silk scarf and was
last seen wearing jeans and a gray sweatshirt. If any-
body spots her, report it directly to Washington. Fast.
A diplomatic problem."

"Confidential?"

"Absolutely. There was also a female Muslim federal agent, with a dark complexion. She also keeps her head covered. And another Fed, male, who I never saw."

"Likely the whole crowd's dead," the sergeant said flatly.

JASMIN AL-SAID WASN'T DEAD. She was in a tent on Muskrat Island, where the heat was oppressive and insects swarmed around her. Her ankles were still locked in leg irons, and the chain between them was fastened to a long chain by a padlock. The other end of that chain was padlocked to a heavy stake that had been driven into the ground.

Sako Takahashi had been furious with the men who left the body of the federal agent in his car. The other two had been shot on the island, and their bodies were buried in the sandy soil. Jasmin wondered why Takahashi hadn't killed her, too.

So did Steiner.

"She's a witness," he said to the Japanese. "A minor witness but a witness."

Steiner sat in the shade of another tent and got the benefit of the breeze that blew off the river. He wore khaki shorts and no shirt. His upper body was wrapped in a bandage that was wet with sweat and grimy with dust. With every breath, his cracked rib sent a sharp pain up his body. The mosquitoes and flies that swarmed around him added to his agony.

"Keppler will want to know," he added.

"She's mine," the Japanese said. "A bonus. I intend to return her to her father for a large fortune."

"You might need a fortune," Steiner stated. "So far, all you have produced is a hole in the ground." He swept his arm toward the magazine Takahashi had his men building. "And it's useless. We don't need to store our explosives underground."

"*I* will make those decisions," Takahashi said sharply.

"In any case," Steiner persisted, "you don't have any explosives."

A young Palestinian had arrived on the island before dawn, bringing word of the explosion that sank the *Sterling Bradbury*. He had wept as he told how Najati Zuabi and four others had been killed.

"Your great hole must be about finished," Steiner taunted.

"When will you be ready to do something besides sit around and complain?" Takahashi asked. He was getting tired of the German and looked forward to eliminating him, too, when this mission was complete.

"The sooner the better. You're an excellent surgeon."

"I have learned to bind wounds," the Japanese dryly said. "I propose a division of the labor. My chief concern right now is that we seem to have acquired a formidable enemy. You and Keppler take responsibility for eliminating him. I'll get the explosives together and execute our assault on the dam. It's better for all if we don't get in each other's way."

A PENCIL-THIN PROP JET with an American flag on its fin and the words United States of America on the fuselage landed at the Wood County airport, about halfway between Marietta and Parkersburg. It didn't taxi to the terminal, but stopped well out on the ramp, beyond a score of parked private planes. A black-and-white sheriff's car drove out on the ramp and stopped beside the airplane.

Mack Bolan boarded the plane as his friend Hal Brognola rose from behind a small desk. They shook hands.

"So far, so good, Striker," Brognola said. "We still don't know what was saved when that load of dynamite went off, but it didn't do much harm."

"We've lost three agents," Bolan said grimly. "Plus a damn good man—a deputy—lost his leg."

"I'm sorry about Gill Mayo," Brognola said, "but there's some good news. The President received another message from the Green and Black. We haven't paid the hundred million they demand, so they threatened another demonstration. I think you might have prevented that, big guy. Green and Black has got to be frustrated."

"They're dangerous Hal," Bolan said. "Sako Takahashi and Kurt Steiner together in the same gang. It spells very serious trouble."

Brognola pulled out a cigar, unwrapped it and stuck the stogie into a corner of his mouth. "Do you have any idea how they found Princess Jasmin and our people?"

"No idea."

"They want a hundred million dollars for her," Brognola told him. "That was another message to the President. If the emir of Qatar finds out that the United States not only let her be kidnapped but also refused to pay the ransom, not only do we have a serious diplomatic crisis, but an economic one, as well. The emir's got his fingers in a lot of oil over there."

"They work damn fast," said Bolan. "They've only had the girl a few hours."

"I'd say they've got at least one man in Washington, because the ransom demand came from a phone booth there."

"Have you got anything else for me?"

"Unfortunately not. But I want to set you up a local contact. We've taken over a farmhouse a few miles out of town. It's guarded, and it's got communications equipment. The guys I've got installed there know who you are and will work with you. And they've got a small arsenal that's at your disposal. Stay independent, but use the help they can give you."

"Fine."

"I'll feed intel to you through the farmhouse. We figure that the Green and Black will be looking for more explosives. If we hear of any big heists or of any big purchases that are out of the ordinary, anywhere in the country, we'll let you know."

"What about Jasmin?" Bolan asked.

"For now, she's got to be a secondary concern," Brognola replied.

"I also need to hide my witness."

"The girl from the bowling alley? Take her to the farmhouse."

"No, DAMMIT!"

Donna refused to go to the farmhouse.

While Bolan was with Brognola at the airport, Donna had spent the time pacing around the hotel room. She hated being cooped up, and she hated the new clothes that had been bought for her by Sheriff McGraw's wife. They were new and stiff, and contributed to her irritability.

"I want my own clothes, Mike," she said to Bolan. "How dangerous can it be to go to my room and pick them up?"

"Plenty. Those guys will kill you the first chance they get."

She sighed loudly. "I'm sick of being a prisoner. I'll go where you want if I can pick up my stuff."

The house was a big, white framed structure and was nearly a hundred years old. It had a wide porch across the front, where an elderly lady sat in a swing chair cooling herself with a fan. Mrs. Thorn the landlady, lazily watched the traffic roll by on the brick-paved street.

"I don't allow gentlemen to go to girls' rooms," she said emphatically to Bolan.

The warrior sat down on the porch rail and waited for Donna to retrieve her belongings. He, too, watched the street—but with the sharp eye of a soldier.

"Where's she going?" the woman asked accusingly.

"Not to spend any time with me, I promise you," Bolan replied, amused. "I'm just her driver. She's going to visit family."

"Mike!"

The scream came from inside the house, and this time Bolan didn't wait for permission. He ran through the front door and up the stairs. Donna was waiting for him in the hall. The room had been ransacked. Her clothes were scattered around, the drawers were torn out of her dresser and the bed had been ripped apart.

"Where's your damned farm?" Donna asked bitterly.

"Gather up what you can and hurry," Bolan directed.

Mrs. Thorn had followed him up the stairs and now stood outside Donna's room, her face a mask of shock.

"Call Sheriff McGraw," Bolan said to her.

Donna took only two or three minutes to shove some clothes into a duffel bag. Bolan led her back down the wide front stairs into the once-elegant formal front hall, leaving the trembling landlady on the upstairs landing.

"I don't know how long I'll be gone," Donna shouted up to her. Then turning to Bolan said, "What? A week?"

Bolan started to answer her, then abruptly stopped. A car was parked across the street, where none had been parked when they arrived.

"Mrs. Thorn," he said, "do you recognize that Pontiac over there?"

The landlady descended the stairs and frowned.

Bolan spoke firmly to Donna. "Take her down to the basement and don't move until I come for you."

"Why, I'm not going to the cellar!" Mrs. Thorn declared indignantly. "You—"

Bolan drew his Beretta.

"Oh!"

The cellar door was in the hall, and Donna led the muttering landlady to it, then followed her down the steps.

Bolan walked into the living room and looked out the front window, concealing himself behind the curtains. No one sat in the Pontiac, and the street looked deserted.

The rear. If the Pontiac had carried any hostiles, then they'd probably gone around behind the house. Staying below window level, the Executioner walked through the living room and into the kitchen.

Peering cautiously through a small window above the sink, he saw no one in the backyard. But there was a garage along the alley that ran behind the house, and through one of its windows Bolan could see bright reflections of the chrome grille of the car inside. Then, abruptly, those reflections disappeared for an instant.

Someone was in the garage and had walked between the car and the window. The warrior waited a minute to make sure that the person made no move to open the doors. Satisfied that the stranger wasn't there to take out the car, he crossed the kitchen and entered a pantry, where the window looked out on the other side of the house. No one was between the houses. Back in the kitchen, he stared at the garage.

The side door opened and a man stepped out. He was carrying two sticks of dynamite taped together, with a yard-long pigtail of fuse hanging down and sparking, issuing thick white smoke.

"No!"

A woman screamed from the back porch of the next house.

The man with the bomb hesitated for an instant, then looked behind him. A second man had come out of the garage, carrying an automatic. He swung the muzzle toward the porch and fired a shot.

The man with the dynamite trotted forward, then took a stance and cocked his arm behind him to throw the bomb at Mrs. Thorn's house.

Bolan fired his Beretta through the window above the kitchen sink. The slug punched through the glass, straight into the bomber's face.

The man fell back, dead, and dropped the dynamite in the middle of a patch of lettuce. The second man jumped to grab it. He snatched it up and got set to throw. Bolan's next shot slammed into the second hardman's chest, knocking him down with the bomb still in his hand.

And there, a moment later, it went off. It tore the man's body to pieces, gouged a crater in the ground and destroyed the garden. The concussion of the blast blew in the wall of the garage and shattered the windows in the houses to both sides of the alley.

Bolan ran outside. The neighbor stood shrieking on her back porch. She hadn't been hit, but she stood in the litter of soil and debris that had been thrown against her house by the blast.

"Down, lady, down!" he yelled. "It might not be over."

And it wasn't. A black Mercury roared up the alley. Bolan vaulted the rail of Mrs. Thorn's back porch and dropped to the ground in a combat crouch.

The Beretta was leveled and ready even before the Mercury screeched to a stop. A man in the front seat rested an Uzi on the door and took aim. Just as he spotted the Executioner crouched at the base of the porch and began to adjust his aim, a 9 mm slug took him out with a chest shot.

Bolan understood that their idea had been to blast the house and take out Donna and him with a burst of gunfire as they fled. That meant there was probably someone covering the front of the house.

The warrior sprang to his feet and was on the porch in a second. As he entered the kitchen, another gunner moved through the front door. The two men saw each other and swung up their weapons almost simultaneously. It was accuracy rather than speed that won the showdown. As a burst from the Uzi ripped into the kitchen wall, the Executioner's lethal slug found its mark in the gunner's heart.

STRICTLY SPEAKING it hadn't been a farmhouse for many years. It had been the home of a slightly eccentric college professor who had enjoyed playing at gentleman farmer. Most of the two hundred acres had been allowed to grow up in weeds and brush. Once consisting of a dozen outbuildings, all but the farmstead's house and barn had been allowed to fall down. Those two buildings, though, were in good repair. In fact, the barn had been converted into a dormitory for students who had once made the professor's "farm" into a sort of commune.

The house and barn were well situated for what Brognola's covert team meant to do. It stood at the top of a low hill, with a clear view of every approach, thus making it easily defensible. The loft in the barn lent itself to the installation of communications equipment. Dish antennas were invisible to passersby, and all the team's vehicles could be pulled inside the one-time milking room of the barn.

The team leader was named Brad Updike. "Hal hopes both of you will move in," he said.

"You got us, for the time being," Bolan replied.

Updike led them into the kitchen of the farmhouse, where a pot of coffee was steaming on the stove. "The town's in an uproar," Updike said. "We've been monitoring their police radio. The mayor called the governor asking for National Guard troops. You two were on the town's most-wanted list for a while this afternoon. A call from Washington cooled that."

"The Guard couldn't solve their problem," said Bolan. "The town's the center of Green and Black activities. They've got to have an arsenal and a barracks someplace close. I need to know where."

"We're working on it," Updike replied. "The moment we've got it pinpointed, we'll let you know."

Bolan nodded. "Make sure the girl's safe," he said. "I'm going back into town tonight."

AT 7:30 HE WALKED into the dining room in the Lafayette Hotel, sat down and ordered a bourbon and soda. A little earlier he'd changed into suitable dinner clothes and, carrying a leather attaché case, checked "Rance Pollock" out of the second hotel. It would have been difficult to guess that the warrior's blue blazer concealed a 9 mm Beretta riding in finely tooled leather under his left arm.

As Bolan had expected, the bulgy-eyed "Texan," Keppler, was at dinner, too. He'd identified the man as a potential hostile during his first visit. But it wasn't easy to figure. The man was handsomely dressed and sat with a bottle of wine on his table—which he obviously meant to drink. He glanced up and noticed that Bolan had come in.

A moment after being seated, the hostess came to Bolan's table and told him the gentleman from Texas, Mr. Johnson, was inviting Mr. Belasko to join him.

Well, this was one way to learn if his suspicions were correct. If they were, Bolan thought, the guy had nerve. He smiled and nodded at the man and rose to move to his table.

"Eating alone night after night is dull, don't you agree?" the man said. "My name is Ben Johnson."

"Mike Belasko."

"Well, I appreciate your joining me. I'm in the oil business, Mr. Belasko—"

"Mike."

"Mike. Of course. Thank you. And I'm Ben. I'm here looking into the possibility of doing some secondary-recovery work in this area. You know, going back to old oil friends to see if you can squeeze any more out of them."

"I lease coal land," Bolan said.

"Ah, yes. A related business."

"They say you're a Texan. Frankly you don't sound Texan."

Keppler laughed. "My *company* is in Texas," he said. "But as you might have guessed, my background's German."

"Are you in town for long, Ben?"

"A week or two. There are those in town who think I'm going to be their salvation, bring back prosperity to old oil fields. Actually we might attempt very modest operations here."

The waitress came to take an order. Keppler remarked that the veal scaloppine he was eating was quite good, but Bolan ordered a steak and fries.

"The river is everything to this town, the whole area, I suppose," Bolan said.

"Yes. All of middle America depends on the rivers for its prosperity. They carry the lifeblood of the nation's economy—as the Rhine does for Western Europe.

Bolan stared at the man across the table. "Thank God rivers can't be blocked," he said.

Keppler put his wineglass to his lips. "Yes...Thank God."

For an hour the two men sat and chatted casually. Bolan gradually came to realize that Keppler *wanted* him to know that he was a key to the Green and Black, and along with Takahashi and Steiner, a source of all the trouble that was spoiling the river valley.

But simple arrogance didn't seem to be his motive. Bolan had seen enough of that in the Mafia dons. It had often been precisely that arrogance that had made them careless—and ultimately dead. No, the heavyset man opposite him wasn't that sort. Bolan judged him as a man who wanted to meet his adversary before disposing of him.

The Executioner could have struck a major blow then and there by taking out this German with the Beretta. But he wouldn't have learned anything more.

"The very best of luck to you, Mike," Keppler said as he signed the check he'd insisted on taking. "I hope we can do this again if both of us are in town long."

"Well, thank you, Ben. I'd like to sign the check once, anyway."

The warrior took the elevator to his room, leaving "Ben Johnson" smoking a cigar over his third cup of coffee and second snifter of brandy.

During their dinner, the German hadn't left the table, and therefore couldn't have made a call. He might, though, have sent a signal to someone. Bolan took no chances. He unlocked his room, then shoved the door back with his foot. Beretta in hand, he entered the hotel room and checked it. It was clean.

For now.

Something would be coming down before long, and he meant to be ready.

The attaché case didn't hold papers. He'd come from the farmhouse with some of the tools of his deadly trade. Bolan stripped and in a moment was dressed in his blacksuit. Plastic armor shielded his torso, and weapons and tools hung on a web belt around his waist.

He had the Desert Eagle, and the Beretta, which he now fitted with its suppressor and loaded with subsonic ammo. He had a Bali-Song, perhaps the deadliest combat knife ever made. As well, he had a coil of nylon rope, a flashlight and one concussion grenade.

The Executioner had come back into town tonight to dare them—and he was ready for the game.

Turning off the lights in his room, but leaving on the light in the bathroom, he opened the window and climbed out onto the ledge. Looping the nylon rope around a steam pipe under the window, he carefully lowered himself until he hung suspended below it. Then, the warrior reached up and pulled the window down, almost shut.

He lowered himself to the ground, then yanked at the rope until it fell. The room was left with a window an inch open, but no one in it.

Now the warrior slipped around to the rear of the hotel, entered through a back door and climbed the rear stairs to the top floor. He knew the hotel wasn't full—it hadn't been since he'd checked in—and took a chance that the room above his wasn't occupied. He used a thin blade to open the door and went in to find it vacant.

So far so good.

Bolan locked the door and fastened the security chain. Crossing, he opened the window just above the one he'd climbed out.

He tied the rope to the radiator and once again lowered himself. He hooked his ankles around the rope above and hung upside down, letting himself down until he could see through his window.

In the light shining through the bathroom door, he could see that no one had entered.

Knowing that they'd wait for him to go to sleep, he climbed back up the rope and sat down on the roof of the hotel.

The river lay below, wide and dark. He could see for miles downstream and a mile or so upstream. Overhead an airplane passed quietly, its red and green navigation lights blinking. Below, on the street, people laughed. The shootings didn't seem to have kept them at home. If anything, the street seemed as busy as ever.

Twenty minutes after his first try, Bolan let himself down headfirst to check the window to his room again. It was dark. Someone had either switched off the bathroom light, or closed the door.

Bolan wasn't ready to risk sticking his head too far down to see into the room, because the dim light outside would silhouette him against the sky.

Suddenly the window was shoved up. A man's head poked out and peered around. It didn't occur to him to look up. The Executioner was less than three feet above him.

"He didn't come out the goddamned door," said a voice inside the room.

"Then he must have gone out the window," another voice replied.

The first man stuck his head even farther out and looked all around.

Bolan drove the blade of the Bali-Song into the side of his neck. The man made no sound as he slumped over, balanced on the windowsill.

The warrior didn't wait for a reaction from inside the room. With the speed of a cat, he climbed back up to the room above, disappearing inside the window just as two shots from a silenced pistol whipped up the wall.

They'd figured it out fast, and unless they were scared, they'd be coming up after him. They'd know that he was either in the room above his own, or on the roof.

Aware that he could be trapped in the room, Bolan went out into the hall. The elevator would be the worst trap of all, and going down the rope from another room—even for a half a minute—would mark him for easy target practice.

But Bolan had planned the attack thoroughly. The steel door at the end of the hall led to the roof. Drawing the killers there would ensure both that the battle would be on his turf, and that no innocents would be in the line of fire.

Passing through the door and shutting it after him, Bolan could hear their footsteps coming up the stairs from the floor below. He heard the muffled crack of shots as the gunmen punctured the door at the top of the stairs before opening it.

The black-clad warrior climbed up a set of steel steps that led to a wedge-shaped wooden shack on the roof. Except for ventilation pipes that rose at intervals, the roof was a wide-open space, unobstructed, with no place to hide.

The Executioner didn't intend to hide.

Taking a place facing the door in the stairway shack, he drew the Desert Eagle and readied it in his hand.

But the men were trained killers and weren't about to burst out onto the roof into the face of Bolan's fire.

For what seemed like a long time they hesitated on the steps.

Then a grenade rolled out onto the roof toward Bolan—an apple of death that would loose a storm of steel pellets he couldn't survive.

The Executioner's only chance was to snap off a shot from the Desert Eagle. The high-velocity .44 Magnum slug blew the grenade apart. It went off, but the rupturing of the case an instant before it exploded dissipated the bulk of the force of the explosion. With the shell shattered, the charge exploded in open air, and much of the energy of the blast was wasted as noise and flash.

A chunk of the shell struck Bolan hard in the stomach. Its impact was taken by his plastic vest. Another chunk of death tore into his thigh, ripping his combat suit and boring into hard muscle. The pain was sharp, but not disabling.

Believing their grenade had taken out their enemy, two men dashed recklessly onto the roof—into two quick shots from the Desert Eagle.

8

At the farmhouse, Brad Updike was busy stitching Bolan's injured thigh.

"That's a nasty little wound there, soldier," he said. "You're lucky that piece of shrapnel didn't hit an artery."

Bolan nodded. He'd been relaying everything he knew about a "Ben Johnson" from Texas to the Justice agent.

"He's a key player," Bolan stated. "I need to know how and where he fits in."

"We'll get right on it. In the meantime, both you and that leg could use some rest."

The warrior knew that Updike was right on both counts. They *would* get right on it. With Brognola's connections in the intelligence community, the Executioner had one of the world's most sophisticated information-gathering networks behind him. He hoped that after a couple hours' sleep they'd have something for him.

He went upstairs. Like last night, Donna was asleep in the bed where he was supposed to sleep. This time, however, there was an extra cot in the room. The warrior quietly undressed and lay down.

After a short, dreamless sleep he was awakened by a knock on the door. Donna cursed and told whoever it was to go away, but Bolan was alert instantly and asked who was there.

"Brad Updike. Got a message for you. There's been a hit on a mine explosives shed in Pennsylvania."

Bolan rolled off the bed and pulled on his pants. In the gray light just before dawn, he walked to the barn with Updike. In the loft, a crew of one man and one woman worked the telecommunications equipment. A teletype chattered. The woman picked up a yellow teletype that had come in earlier and handed it to Bolan.

It was a message from Brognola.

MINING EXPLOSIVES COMPANY HIT SHORTLY AFTER MIDNIGHT. FOUR MILES SOUTH OF MATHER, PA. THREE DEAD. LARGE QUANTITY OF EXPLOSIVES BELIEVED MISSING. POSSIBLY BEING TRANSPORTED THROUGH PITTSBURG, THEN DOWN OHIO RIVER. DO NOT ATTEMPT TO INTERCEPT UNLESS IN YOUR VICINITY. CONVINCED TERRORIST ATTACK PLANNED MARIETTA-PARKERSBURG-POMEROY-GALLIPOLIS AREA. OTHERS COVERING SECONDARY DANGER AREAS. YOU ARE AT AREA CONSIDERED MOST DANGEROUS. TAKE SPECIAL CARE.

                                        HAL

Updike pointed to a map thumbtacked to the wall. A pin had been stuck in at Mather, Pennsylvania.

"Assuming those explosives were put aboard a boat," he said, "it would take two or three days for them to arrive here."

"In trucks they could be here in six or seven hours. Maybe less."

Donna, still sleepy and peevish, had ambled into the communications center carrying two mugs of hot black coffee. She stared at the map for a minute, then said, "Why take the stuff on a boat all the way up around the north part of the river, a hundred miles out of their way? Once you get south of Wheeling, the river traffic's much heavier. There's ten times as many barges to look at, and they all come through every lock on the river." She shrugged. "You aren't *ever* going to find that dynamite."

Bolan looked at her, frowning. She had no place in the communications center. He'd have told her just that, had she not known what she was talking about.

"What kind of barge would they use?"

"Probably a container barge," she replied, "loaded with sealed containers. To find something they don't want you to find, you'd have to open thousands of them. Even if you found the right one, it would be packed with five hundred cartons of say, auto parts. And fifty only of those cartons would have dynamite in them."

Bolan shot a glance at Updike.

"We're on it," the man from Justice said.

DONNA DOW WAS CORRECT. The Green and Black had planned to move the explosives farther downriver by land, hoping that once it was on the water, it would be overlooked by the authorities along with the millions of tons of cargo already on the busy waterway.

They'd moved quickly. Within an hour of the heist, the explosives had been loaded on a semi in two medium-size containers and transported south into Ohio.

By dawn the semi arrived at Powhatan Point, sixty miles northeast of Marietta. It waited on a wharf with a row of other trucks as a huge crane swung its cargo onto a container barge.

The tow was in sight. It eased up to the wharf, and deckhands leaped to connect the container barge to the rest of the tow. Ten minutes later, the *Charles Monroe* was churning out into the river and moving downstream.

JASMIN AL-SAID CRAWLED OUT of her tent, as the rising sun began to heat it like an oven. She was still chained to the post and found it difficult to find a private place to relieve herself. Her sense of dignity had been violated many times since being held on the island, and her problems now only contributed to her misery.

After she'd finished, a man crawled across the sandy ground toward her. He was Palestinian and had spoken to her in Arabic several times previously. During those meetings she'd spoken of God, but he'd laughed.

As he approached her, his great toothy grin left little doubt about what he wanted.

She didn't speak. She only shook her head.

Crawling closer still, the Palestinian rose to his knees, and kneeling, began to open his pants.

Jasmin continued to shake her head as tears ran down her cheeks. She didn't cry out. What good would it do in this camp of depraved savages?

Then like a flash, a steel object darted through the air and into the Palestinian's throat. He choked as his eyes bulged, and he toppled forward.

Jasmin had no idea what had hit the menacing Palestinian, nor who had thrown it. In fact, it was a metal throwing star, with eight razor-sharp points. Whipping silently through the air, it had cut through the man's windpipe as effectively as the stroke of a knife.

Sako Takahashi stepped into the clearing. He snapped his fingers, and a man trotted out after him. With a curt gesture, he was ordered to dispose of the Palestinian's still-twitching body. The man—another Japanese—knelt over the Palestinian and shoved a knife into and up the base of his skull. The would-be rapist stopped twitching. Then he was dragged away.

WORD OF THE next explosives theft came almost simultaneously—from Washington and Sheriff Mc-Graw. No one had been killed or injured in the raid, but the construction company's stock of dynamite and blasting gelatin had been stripped clean. Cases of explosives had been carted away.

"Calhoun County," McGraw told Bolan, "is about fifty miles up the Little Kanawha River. The stuff isn't coming here by boat. It's coming by truck."

"They knew where to go and knew what they wanted."

"Damn right. It looks like they've targeted the chief storage facilities in this part of the country. We never had to guard the stuff much before, and it's not easy to start guarding it all now."

Bolan nodded. "Washington thinks it's all coming here."

"Shit. Just what I need."

STEINER WAS WORKING with two liabilities. In the first place, he was still in great pain from the wound he'd suffered two days earlier. Secondly the man he had to kill had seen him and would recognize him.

The town noticed foreigners—unless they were obviously college students—so he couldn't use one of the Palestinians as an errand boy. As well, his accent prevented him from speaking very much. Takahashi understood this and had assigned him a West Virginian by the name of Billy Buckhannon.

Buckhannon wasn't a very bright fellow. Brutish in appearance, he was at no pains to hide the fact that he looked on all foreigners, including Steiner and Takahashi, as inferior to an American like himself. He'd done time in the penitentiary for armed robbery and time in the Parkersburg jail for assault.

He drove an old green pickup, its paint all but hidden under a coat of mud. In the glove compartment he carried a stainless-steel .357 Magnum Smith & Wesson revolver. Behind the seat of the pickup, in a clutter of trash, he also kept a 12-gauge double-barrel shotgun. It had been sawed, so it had only about ten inches of barrel and no stock.

Steiner knew he couldn't return to the Lafayette Hotel. Buckhannon checked him into a modest little motel behind a service station on the north edge of town. He paid cash in advance, as the station owner required, and settled down in a tiny room only half cooled by a rattling window air conditioner.

"First thing we do is find the big man," Steiner said to Buckhannon.

"You mean you don't even know where the son of a bitch is? Where are we supposed to start?"

"We get him to come to us," the German said, coolly. "A little trap. But first, I've got an errand for you."

AN HOUR LATER, Buckhannon walked into a village hardware store and told the proprietor he needed enough dynamite to blast out a tree stump. One stick would probably do it, but he'd take two to be sure.

The proprietor required him to sign in a ledger and to show his driver's license for identification. Billy had expected this and produced a Pennsylvania driver's license in the name Tom Sneed. He'd stolen it during a mugging some months earlier and was pleased to be able to use it now.

Some time later, the two sticks of dynamite went off in a drifting skiff on the Ohio River a few miles downstream from Parkersburg. When Sheriff Mc-Graw arrived, Mack Bolan was with him. Steiner watched through powerful binoculars as Bolan and the sheriff walked along the riverbank.

"I don't get this," McGraw said. "All I can figure is that somebody made a mistake and blew himself up."

Bolan stood looking at the river. Two boats were working, dragging grappling hooks along the bottom, trying to find a body. Except for that, and the people who'd come out for a look, the river showed no sign of the explosion.

Witnesses described the blast as powerful, but there was no way to tell how much explosive had gone off. Bolan noticed, though, that it hadn't swept the leaves off trees on the riverbank, had not broken windows in a group of summer cottages along the shore. Add that to the uneasy feeling—call it a survival instinct—he'd had since arriving there, and it started to make sense.

"I think we've been had."

"Huh?"

"Had," Bolan repeated. "It's either a diversion for something bigger coming down, or it's a trap. I think we ought to move out. Let's get back in your car and get on the radio."

"Now we follow them," Steiner said to Buckhannon.

Billy jammed the pickup into gear and rattled out onto the highway. Following the cruiser that carried the Executioner and McGraw, they drove back to Marietta. The black-and-white car entered the parking garage in the basement of the county courthouse.

"We can't hardly shoot him in the sheriff's office, now can we?"

"We wait."

As THE SUN SET, the *Charles Monroe* stopped at a huge wharf just downstream from Marietta and delivered the container barge. Cranes began to lift the containers off and put them on trailers. The first two containers went onto two trucks not designed to carry that kind of load. Nevertheless they fit on the beds and were lashed down.

It wasn't yet dark when the two vehicles left the terminal. The whole business had looked entirely normal and innocent. Thousands of containers a day were moved on and off barges, all up and down the river.

What wasn't innocent was the plans for that cargo.

STEINER AND BUCKHANNON had left the pickup and stationed themselves in the bank parking lot behind the courthouse. After sunset there were only three or four cars parked there. They took positions behind two vehicles and waited for the big man to come out.

Buckhannon's sawed-off shotgun was hidden under the sleeve of his nylon jacket. It hung on a piece of clothesline that was looped around his neck, which enabled him to grab the weapon and fire it in half a second. The .357 Magnum hung in a canvas holster on his right hip. He wore a baseball cap and leaned against an old Buick station wagon, chewing tobacco and spitting.

Steiner had a compact Smith & Wesson 9 mm automatic pistol under his jacket, but his chief weapon—the one he meant to use to take out the big man once and for all—was an Ingram M-10A1, the most recent version of the Model 10. Steiner knew his weapons, which was why he'd chosen this particular gun. The rate of fire had been slowed to give the shooter easier control over the weapon. Fired either as a submachine gun or as a semiautomatic, the Ingram cycled rounds with extraordinary accuracy. This one was chambered for 9 mm rounds.

Steiner was becoming impatient. His cracked rib had begun to throb, and the salt of the sweat under his bandages stung his flesh. Besides that, the bastard seemed likely to stay in the sheriff's office half the night.

In fact, Bolan and McGraw had spent some time going over reports of explosives thefts, of which they'd been two more during the day. As he was ready to leave, McGraw saw the Executioner check his Beretta.

"Where's the big automatic?" the sheriff asked.

"In the car," Bolan replied.

The car he meant was a rented black Ford. It was the one Steiner was huddled behind.

But before the warrior appeared, a city police car swung into the parking lot. It came to a stop with its headlights bearing down on Steiner. The policeman got out and walked toward him.

"That your car?" the cop asked.

Steiner shook his head. He didn't want the policeman to hear his German accent.

"Then what are you doing?"

Steiner shrugged. "Just standing here."

The cop stared at him for a long moment, trying to assess the situation. Steiner had managed to ditch the Ingram under the car, but there was a noticeable bulge under his jacket.

"Turn around and put your hands on top of the car."

The policeman drew his service revolver. He meant business. Steiner turned and put his hands on top of the car, knowing that when the cop began to pat him down he'd immediately find the Smith & Wesson automatic—a concealed weapon.

Steiner was slow to turn around and managed to make a bit of noise by shuffling his feet. It was all the time he needed.

The cop grunted, and in the next second he was down on the pavement of the parking lot. Buckhannon had come up behind him and smashed the butt of his big revolver down on the cop's head.

Mack Bolan shook hands with McGraw and trotted down the steps toward the double glass doors that led to the parking lot.

He noticed the police car with its light flashing, and he stopped. With his hand on the door, Bolan studied the lot. A man stood beside his rented car, and another man was walking away. There was no police officer in sight.

Another man might have walked on out. Kept walking to the lot. For a man with Bolan's life experience, the situation tripped an instinctive alarm. Two men in the parking lot by a police car with no policeman wasn't right. He backed one step away from the doors.

Both Steiner and Buckhannon spotted him, silhouetted in the courthouse lobby's light.

Buckhannon jerked the shotgun from under his jacket, raised the muzzle and fired one barrel. A storm of buckshot flew toward the glass doors, turning them to powder. Luckily they were heavy, stopping all but a few of the lethal pellets.

Bolan threw himself to the floor just as a second hail of buckshot roared through the corridor, ricocheting off walls and tearing away great hunks of plaster. Because the warrior was flat on the floor, the entire charge flew over him.

Jumping up, Bolan ran in a crouch toward the rear of the corridor.

Steiner had retrieved his Ingram from under Bolan's rented car immediately after the policeman was knocked out. Holding it in one hand like a pistol, he loosed a burst of 9 mm rounds toward the smashed doors.

The weapon fired like that, Steiner didn't get the accuracy the submachine gun was capable of. His burst went high, chewing away part of the ceiling and putting out most of the lights in the corridor.

Bolan raced into a cross hall and kicked open the first door he came upon. It was some sort of storage room, filled mostly with paper boxes piled four or five high. The room was dark except for light shining in from the parking lot, and he rushed across the room to the windows.

Buckhannon reloaded his shotgun as Steiner gestured wildly for him to charge into the courthouse after the big man. Steiner had survived a lot of battles by letting other people go ahead of him, and Billy Buckhannon was willing.

In fact, he was mad. He was so mad, that he had to fight down an impulse to let the German have a load of buckshot, as well. But then who'd pay him? His eyes narrowed as he strode across the parking lot toward the broken doors.

Bolan saw him coming. He recognized Steiner and the Ingram submachine gun. The German was a dangerous man with a dangerous weapon. Bolan would have liked to get a shot off at the man, but the German terrorist was keeping cover behind the car.

Buckhannon charged through the doors and into the corridor. Pulling his .357 Magnum, he took a quick look into the cross hall and saw the open door into the storage room.

Bolan heard him storming through the courthouse and readied himself. The last thing he wanted was to be pinned down between the open door and the window.

Buckhannon jumped through the door from the hall and threw himself to one side. He fired both barrels of his shotgun, one a little to his left, the other to his right, and the room was virtually filled with the spraying buckshot.

It tore through the stacked paper cartons and ripped into a wooden desk and the steel sides of the filing cabinets. Half a dozen ricocheting pellets stung Bolan on the legs.

Steiner saw the muzzle-flashes from the parking lot. He leveled the Ingram on the closest window and fired a long burst. Maybe he'd kill Buckhannon, but he didn't care.

Bolan hoped he would. The warrior could have easily taken out the brutish West Virginian himself had the Ingram not been a factor. He was, in fact, under one of the windows, crouched low enough to be out of the line of Steiner's fire. It had just taken out most of the room's back wall, but missed Buckhannon. With the Beretta set to fire 3-round bursts, Bolan still didn't have a shot.

McGraw and two deputies came running down the hall. Steiner didn't know they were there, but when he fired another burst through the window, the slugs broke through the rear wall of the room and drove the sheriff and his men back.

"Crazy damn bastard!"

Buckhannon fired a shot from his .357 Magnum, which tore through cartons of paper and plowed into the plaster wall two feet from Bolan.

The Executioner had had enough. The time had come to move.

He rose and fired a 3-round burst. The muzzle-flash was hidden and gave Buckhannon nothing to aim at. Nevertheless, he swung around and fired at where he thought he'd heard Bolan's gunfire coming from, missing by two feet.

The Executioner now had a target. He fired another burst and saw the shadowy figure jerk, then drop, with his big pistol clattering on the floor.

Turning his attention to Steiner, Bolan poked his head in the window just enough to take a look.

The police car was moving toward the parking lot's exit.

Bolan held his fire. There was no way to be positive that it was Steiner escaping in the police car. He could kill a police officer, and that was a chance he wouldn't take. The Executioner cursed to himself as the vehicle screeched into the street and sped away.

A FLATBOAT DREW UP to a small barge terminal. It was a sturdily built wooden vessel, twenty-five feet long, and was driven by a Chevrolet engine. The wharf crew paid little attention to the three men who presented their papers and opened the shipping containers.

Even if they'd closely watched the three men remove the boxes and stack them on the flatboat, they wouldn't have known that they contained dynamite.

Everything was in order. Flatboats constantly made small deliveries to businesses that couldn't afford big wharfs. The little boat moved out onto the river and headed toward the West Virginia shore. It crossed over sunken gravel bars that would have hung up bigger tows, and churned in a southeastern direction toward Muskrat Island.

The pilot switched off the navigation lights and pushed the flatboat onto the island. Holding its nose against the bank with the idling engine, he waited while a score of men scrambled on board and carried off the wooden cases.

Sako Takahashi watched with satisfaction as the sweating men carried cases of dynamite into the underground bunker that had finally been completed. He now had more than he'd lost in the blast of the *Sterling Bradbury*—and the big man in Marietta hadn't discovered it or interfered.

9

"I have a favor to ask you," Sheriff McGraw said the next morning. "There's some people I want you to talk to."

Because the farmhouse used by Justice was in Washington County, Hal Brognola had decided Jack McGraw should know about it. He sat now at a table with Mack Bolan, Brad Updike and Donna Dow. McGraw had asked no questions, but by now he was sure that "Mike Belasko" wasn't an officer with the West Virginia State Police and was probably associated in some way with the Justice Department. Meeting Brad Updike only confirmed it.

"*I* can't meet anybody, Sheriff," Updike replied. "You absolutely must not let the word out that anyone from Washington, D.C., is here."

"I didn't tell these people they'd be meeting anyone from the federal government," McGraw said. "Frankly I've got a committee of vigilantes forming, and I'd like to head it off some way. If they don't get some assurance, innocent people are going to get killed."

Updike looked at Bolan. "Maybe you can do it."

"How would I be introduced?" Bolan asked.

Updike frowned at McGraw. "You've already got part of it figured out, haven't you, Sheriff? Mike Belasko isn't a West Virginia officer, but he's not a federal agent, either. He's a specialist at fighting terrorism and he has a lot of experience at it."

"My vigilantes want to stop the drug pushers."

"He's got a lot of experience with drug dealers," Updike said. "He's taken out a lot of them."

McGraw spoke to Bolan. "You could maybe save some lives if you'll talk to these men."

An hour later the sheriff led Bolan through a general store in the village of Watertown and into a back room where half a dozen men were meeting. Bolan had been a little apprehensive about the meeting during the drive over. Talking down a group of vigilantes just wasn't the warrior's strong suit, but saving innocent peoples' lives was. He'd always been willing to do it in any way possible.

McGraw introduced him as a specialist in fighting drug dealers and told them to listen to what he had to say.

"Let us tell you something first," said a big, sunburned man named Floyd Varner. "Three, four months ago my son was everything a man could want. Now, it's like he's burned out. All he can think of is how to get another hit of cocaine. He'll steal to get the money for it, and I honest to God believe he'd kill for it. He's stolen from his mother and me, shoplifted in stores. We've begged him, and we've beat him. Anything to stop him." Varner shook his head. "We don't know what to do."

"Least..." another man started to say, then stopped and closed his eyes. He couldn't go on.

"What Sherman is trying to tell you," Varner said, "is that his sixteen-year-old daughter has been doing things to get the stuff that no girl should have to."

"What we want to know," Sherman Phelps muttered, struggling to keep his voice under control, "is what's being done. 'Cause if we don't get some help, we ain't got not choice but to do what we can."

"What do you think you can do?" Bolan asked grimly.

"It's plain," one of the farmers said. "Down the river here a couple weeks ago, a man hauling cocaine in a sack took a couple of rifle shots in the back. The stuff ain't as easy to get down his way now."

Bolan nodded. "I read you, and I'm with you, too. But you're dealing with killers. And they're armed."

"That shooting at the courthouse last night," Jack McGraw said. "Those guys were trying to kill Mr. Belasko. They fired a submachine gun at him. The shooting on Front Street, the shooting on the roof of the hotel—same guys, same idea. The bombing on Fourth Street was more of the same thing. Only that time they weren't trying to kill Mike. They were after a witness."

"Maybe you need help," one of the men said to Bolan.

The warrior grinned. "Maybe I do. But you've got wives and kids," he said. "I'd like to make a suggestion. Let the pros take the heat. If you go after these people, sooner or later some of you are going to get killed. They've got military weapons, and they don't care who they hurt."

The farmers exchanged glances. "Something's already happened," Varner said. "The fat guy from the service station, Bart, has been selling to the kids. But they won't buy it from him no more. Seems like a stray shot got him while he was buying some of the stuff. You'll find him on Township 8 along with the fella who was bringing it to him."

McGraw shook his head. "You shouldn't have done it," he said unhappily. "You can't solve anything—"

"Oh, I didn't do it," Varner told him. "And I got no idea who did."

"Nobody's reported it," McGraw said.

"I just did. Otherwise they'd both just rot there. Nobody would call the law. That's how we feel about it."

The mood of the room was starting to heat up, and Bolan was concerned. "What are you people going to do when they come after you?" he asked.

"Come after us?" Varner asked. "After who?"

"After your town. If they decide to kill somebody out here, to teach your town a lesson, they'll kill anybody. They don't care if they get the man who took out their man. Anybody will do."

"Maybe they won't know where it happened. Or how."

"Don't count on that," Bolan replied. "They know where they sent their man. When he doesn't come back—"

"Maybe they'll think *you* did it," one of the farmers suggested.

Bolan nodded. "Maybe they will."

"No," Varner stated. "If we made a problem, then *we've* got to fix it. We don't put it on another man's head."

"I guess we know what we've got to do," Sherm Phelps announced.

SELLING DRUGS IN THE TOWNS along the river was the way the Green and Black was financing its ambitious scheme to blast out a dam. Sako Takahashi had assembled the gang using a variety of recruiting methods. For the most fanatic, the chance to stroke a telling blow against the "Great Satan" was enough. But for many others, it was the promise of great wealth by opening up a new drug market that had convinced them to take risks that were increasing every day. Even with that inducement, a dozen men had deserted the Green and Black in the past few days. They simply walked away, saying they'd never signed on to fight the kind of man opposing them this past week. Some locals—Ohioans, West Virginians, Kentuckians—who had signed on for the money, just disappeared.

On the island, Takahashi had killed a Palestinian who tried to desert. To the Japanese, a man who tried to abandon his cause, once he'd committed himself to it, deserved nothing less than death.

Despite its problems the Green and Black was still a well-organized group. Takahashi was in charge of the main thrust of its operation: getting the explosives and preparing the scheme for getting them into a river lock. Steiner was assigned perhaps the most difficult task, which was to take out the warrior. Keppler had inherited supervision of the drug operation. On the phone to big suppliers in New York and Florida, he was importing greater quantities of purer stuff and was improving distribution.

So it was to Gerd Keppler that word came that the man sent out to deliver a supply of cocaine and crack to Watertown hadn't returned. That man was no traitor. He was a Syrian they called Big Mahmoud, a man with a record of loyalty and effectiveness. If he didn't return, someone had hit him. Maybe it was to steal his stuff, maybe retaliation from outraged farmers from the village. Or maybe it was the big warrior. Whichever way it was, it couldn't be ignored.

Before returning to the Lafayette Hotel early in the afternoon, Keppler stopped at a small motel where one of the lieutenants of the Green and Black was staying. He ordered him to assemble some troops and find the yellow Toyota that Big Mahmoud had been driving.

"If they killed him," he said maliciously, "do something to make them wish they hadn't."

The man in charge of the six-man team was Angelo Dioguardi, an Italian and a veteran of the Red Brigades. He was forty-two years old and had been a professional terrorist since he was eighteen. His face was too well-known in Italy for him to function there anymore, so he'd spent the past seven years in the States.

"He'd been given two cars—a gray Pontiac, and a white Cutless—with which to take the troops to Watertown. The team included: another Italian, a Lebanese, a Jordanian and two Palestinians. He would rather have had Europeans, because the Arabs were too conspicuous. For this deal, though, it didn't make much difference what they looked like. If they found their man dead, what they were going to do could be done just as well by any men who had the right spirit.

The right spirit, as far as Dioguardi was concerned, was a vengeful readiness to kill.

The two carloads of men drove around the bright green farm-country hills. They saw nothing of the yellow Toyota. They were seen, though, by the farmers, and four separate calls went in to the sheriff's office.

Jack McGraw called the farmhouse and told Bolan about the two cars and the hard-looking men. The Executioner said he'd drive over to Watertown and see what was going on. He suggested that the sheriff not come with deputies unless Bolan called.

Dioguardi decided he wasn't going to find the yellow Toyota. He stopped at the service station, which was still closed, and used the phone booth to call Keppler at the hotel.

"The reason you can't find the Toyota is that it's in the parking lot behind the courthouse—with bullet holes in the windshield. I've seen two hearses. One of them brought in Bart, Mahmoud's drop."

"Which means," Dioguardi concluded, "that the rubes took out Mahmoud, too. Anybody who hit him to steal what he was carrying wouldn't have bothered to take out Bart."

"I accept that reasoning."

"So maybe it's time the rubes learned a lesson."

"Use your own judgment, Angelo."

"They got an old town hall out here. It looks like it's been standing there a hundred years. Bet they'd be sorry to lose it. Some of them might be foolish enough to try to save it."

"Do what you have to do."

WHAT DIOGUARDI DIDN'T understand was that the rubes had been following him in cars and pickups for the past hour. No one vehicle stayed behind the Italian's two cars very long. They switched off. Sherm Phelps followed at one point, Floyd Varner at another, and still others were working the lookout.

Bolan was at the edge of the town, looking for the townspeople he'd met with earlier—and looking for the strangers who had caused the alarm. He'd had no luck so far but knew if he drove around long enough, they'd turn up.

The town hall, Dioguardi had noticed, was a white frame building on a shady square in the center of the tiny village. Dioguardi was right to guess that it was more than the hundred years old and that it was cherished by the residents of the town.

The Firebird and the Cutlass pulled up in front of the town hall, and a man got out of the passenger side of the Olds. It was the second Italian. Dioguardi nodded, and the man loosed a long burst from an Uzi machine pistol into the facade of the little building.

Floyd Varner was half a block up the street, sitting in his pickup and watching through the scope of a .30-.30 deer rifle. When he heard the Uzi stutter and saw wood flying from the front of the town hall, he chambered a round and fired. It found its mark just under the Italian's left shoulder blade. The man sprawled forward on the brick sidewalk in front of the building, screaming and writhing.

Dioguardi threw himself across the front seat of the Firebird and out onto the walk beside the wounded man. He grabbed the Uzi, rose to his knees and rested his arms on the hood of the car. By the time the hardman's blast of 9 mm slugs punched into the pickup, Varner was already out of the vehicle and crouching behind it.

Dioguardi yelled orders, and the rest of his men scrambled out, leveling their weapons at the pickup and opening fire. In seconds Floyd Varner's truck was a shattered wreck, windows blasted out, tires punctured. The big farmer couldn't get off another shot.

Dioguardi thought things were turning out better than he'd expected. Marco was wounded but he was going to take out a rube. Then they'd burn down their damned town hall. He ordered two men to keep the rube down with constant fire, while two others charged him, up both sides of the street.

The Lebanese and one of the Palestinians—the first armed with a Kalashnikov assault rifle, the other just with a .357 Magnum revolver—moved cautiously toward the pickup. Slugs continued to punch through its frame, their impacts rocking the vehicle on its springs.

Dioguardi grinned. They had him all right.

The Lebanese went down with a chest shot that came from behind a Chevrolet farther up the street.

Then, Dioguardi's world fell apart.

MACK BOLAN HAD BEEN driving along a hilly country road and was about to stop in the nearby town to check in with Sheriff McGraw, when he heard the gunfire. He estimated that it came from about half a mile away, and he pressed his foot hard on the accelerator.

Coming up a hill, he spotted the hardmens' cars first, then the pickup a little farther in the distance. There was a crossroad about a quarter mile before the town hall, and Bolan veered his car right, then hard to the left behind the row of tiny wooden buildings that lined the street.

He drove past the hall to the rear of a hardware store. In an instant the Executioner was out of the car, Beretta in hand.

Bolan didn't need to be told which side was which—both the cars and the weapons said it all. The key was to move in on the terrorists before they mowed down the inexperienced farmers.

Moving swiftly to the front of the hardware store, Bolan saw two men, machine guns up and ready, pass before him. He fired at the gunner nearest him, and the shot punched into his chest with a thud.

Bolan readied himself for a second shot, when the Palestinian was swept off his feet by two separate charges of birdshot, fired from a double-barreled shotgun. They'd come from between two houses. In fact, there seemed to be gunfire coming from everywhere.

By now, Dioguardi felt cold fear. He'd come out to this hick town with five good, heavily armed men, and the goddamned rubes had taken down three of them.

The second Palestinian and the Jordanian were obediently pinning down the man behind the pickup. Dioguardi looked at them for a moment, then made a decision. He threw himself across the seat of the Firebird. Holding himself down as much as he could, he started the engine.

The Jordanian and Palestinian understood what they heard. They were being abandoned. To hell with him, they thought. The two men stopped firing on the pickup and jumped into the Cutlass.

Bolan had began to run as soon as he saw the Palestinian go down. He sprinted across the street toward Floyd Varner, just as the farmer squeezed off a carefully aimed shot that killed the Jordanian, who was starting the Olds.

Dioguardi hunched over the steering wheel and shoved the Firebird into gear. He floored the accelerator and swung the car around in a sharp 180-degree turn. With tires shrieking, the Italian began to speed away from the town.

Bolan stood, took aim with the Desert Eagle and fired at the retreating vehicle. His big steel-jacketed slug punched through the rear window of the car, through Angelo Dioguardi and stopped at last in the tachometer.

The Italian wounded by Floyd Varner's first shot rose to his knees with a pistol in his hand. Before the gun was raised, Varner finished him off with a head shot.

The second Palestinian, the last man of the six who'd been sent to Watertown, emerged from the Cutlass, perhaps to surrender. Bolan shouted for the farmers to hold their fire, but he was too late. A shotgun blast from fifteen feet away hurled the man back onto the pavement.

Varner turned and stared at Bolan. The big farmer's face gleamed with sweat, and his eyes were wide. "My God, I killed a man," he said dully.

Bolan glanced around. Other men with guns were walking toward him and Varner, and more people were coming out of their houses and stores, running toward the town hall.

Sherman Phelps approached, carrying the double-barreled shotgun. He'd taken out the last man.

Beyond that, it was difficult for Bolan to tell who'd taken out whom. Several more men emerged in the street carrying various weapons. All of them were awed by what they'd done. Four bodies lay on the street, and two more were slumped behind the wheels of the two cars.

"What have we done?" Varner asked Bolan. "Busted up the drug trade, or bought ourselves a war?"

Bolan shook his head. "I don't know."

JASMIN SAT IN THE SHADE at the entrance to her tent, watching Takahashi talk with the two Germans. Suffering from the stifling heat, she'd abandoned all pretense of modesty and all hope of ever seeing her home again. Although she continued to wear the white scarf on her head, she wore only a pair of white panties and a white bra.

Takahashi had removed her leg irons. The long chain that had once been connected to the stake driven in the ground was now padlocked loosely around her neck.

The conversation between Takahashi and the two Germans was tense, sometimes angry. She wondered what was wrong.

"Dioguardi," the Japanese said bitterly. "Big Mahmoud, Zuabi, Malik and how many more? We're plagued with desertions. And no wonder. They don't trust our leadership any longer."

"We have got to teach those farmers a lesson," Steiner stated.

"No!" Takahashi screamed. He turned on Keppler. "You lost six men this afternoon, trying to teach some stupid farmers a lesson." The Japanese looked truly menacing.

"I remind you," Keppler said calmly, "who's the chairman of the Green and Black."

"And *I* remind *you* that if we don't succeed in blowing up a river lock, there *will* be no Green and Black. Our allies are patient, but their patience won't endure forever."

"How near are you to accumulating enough explosives?" Keppler asked.

The Japanese shrugged. "I have maybe twenty-five percent of what we need. We're mounting a raid tonight on a warehouse in Minnesota where we can get about a ton of dynamite."

"Minnesota? How are you getting it here?"

"By plane, of course. Two planes. Two airports."

Keppler nodded thoughtfully. "You could use, I assume, as much Semtex as I could get you."

Takahashi's chin jerked up, and he showed what was very rare for him—a smile. "The perfect detonator."

"I can't get much," Keppler warned. "And it will cost money. So don't be scornful of our cocaine trade. In fact, I have a plane coming in tonight, bringing another load."

"If you can get the Semtex, that's good," said Takahashi. "However, our chief problem remains that murdering... Well, what can we call him?"

"Der Teufel," Steiner replied. "In English—the Devil."

Takahashi fixed a hard stare on Steiner. "Don't fail again," he said bluntly. "Yours is the easiest assignment. All you have to do is kill one man."

STEINER GUESSED that "the Devil" would somehow learn of the arrival of the shipment of cocaine and crack.

He knew the man now, and he knew he was correct in his guess that the big man would come running to the rescue of the innocent bystanders.

So why take a chance? And why let Keppler's shipment come in unobstructed, making him look like a hero? Steiner was getting sick of constantly being on the firing line, while the bulgy-eyed man sat back and counted the money.

As the sun began to set, Steiner made a decision. He left his motel twenty minutes after Keppler had dropped him off and drove to a telephone booth. He placed a call.

"Sheriff McGraw? A word of advice to you. Be at McConnelsville airport tonight. There'll be a plane full of something that will interest you." Then he hung up.

Steiner knew the big man would show up.

The German was tired of being defeated by the Devil. Defeat was something he'd rarely experienced, and the sharp pain in his ribs only contributed to his silent rage. Tonight he'd be ready.

STEINER ARRIVED at the airport and found it to be as he'd expected—a target range for the weapon he'd assembled.

He walked out onto the field, beyond the ramp, across the paved runway and onto the grass beyond. He wandered around, assessing the terrain. Once satisfied, he sat down, pulled a folding shovel from his kit and began to dig himself a minitrench. He didn't need a foxhole, just a depression in which to lie, where his weapon could be braced and steadily aimed.

The weapon was a Weatherby hunting rifle. Designed for big-game hunting, it was chambered for .460 Magnum ammunition—powerful enough to stop a rhino, let alone a man. The weapon was as much rifle as a strong man could handle. But this one was heavier than usual, because it was equipped with both a night scope and a laser projector. Not only would he be able to see his target in the dark, he'd also be able to aim by putting a dot of red light on the spot where his shot would hit.

Steiner finished digging then stretched out in the depression and set to work to adjust his sights.

"He had a German accent?" Bolan asked.

McGraw nodded. "Our man probably means to get us out of town tonight while something else comes down closer to the river."

"It's possible," Bolan replied, but he doubted it. It just didn't feel right.

"I've got no word of anything else," McGraw told him. "Has anything come in on your space-age antennas?"

Bolan shook his head.

"Well, I've got nothing better to do tonight," the sheriff said.

"Neither do I—except walk into a trap, which is probably what this is all about."

The problem was that the town of McConnelsville wasn't in McGraw's county. He picked up the phone and called Bob Eddy, sheriff of Morgan County. Ten minutes later, Bolan and McGraw went out to meet him.

Like McGraw, Bob Eddy was young, a veteran of military service and a family man. He disliked sitting in an office and welcomed any part of his job that required him to be outside, even if it meant leaving home and going to the airport at night.

Bolan didn't like having to involve other men in what he believed would be a trap set for him by the German terrorist. But if the caller was correct and drugs *were* coming in this night, the sheriff had every right to be there. And if anybody had to be brought in, Bolan's instincts told him that Bob Eddy would be better than many.

McGraw had explained the whole situation to him over the phone, and they reviewed it in the car for the two Morgan County deputies. At Bolan's suggestion they didn't drive directly to the airport, but stopped half a mile away. Out of sight below the crest of the hill, the five men walked up to the landing field.

Bolan scanned the sky. His German-accented caller hadn't suggested the hour when the airplane was supposed to arrive. Bob Eddy was on the radio, checking in with the dispatcher at his office, who would relay to him any word that came by radio or phone from Marietta.

The two sheriffs and the two deputies were armed with rifles as well as their side arms. He himself was carrying both the Desert Eagle and the Beretta. One of the deputies, who had a reputation as something of a marksman, would take out a tire on the airplane— once it was clear that the plane was bringing in narcotics.

Unknown to any of the lawmen, Steiner had been watching them through the Weatherby's scope. The German squirmed in anticipation of the kill. But he was also patient. Several times the big American had passed through his line of sight, and on each occasion another man stepped in the way. Just as he saw his best chance yet, two cars swung in from the road. The drivers didn't see the lawmen until they found themselves staring into the muzzles of their rifles. They came out with their hands up—two drivers and one extra man. The drivers were locals, and McGraw recognized one of them. The extra man was of indeterminate nationality but clearly wasn't a local. All three were handcuffed with their hands behind their backs and put in the hangar.

Bolan had been moving around too much during the commotion for Steiner to get off a shot. Although satisfied with the swiftness with which the drug runners had been apprehended, the warrior couldn't escape the suspicion that tonight was about more than a simple tip-off. The plane would surely be coming soon, but after that...

The airport lights suddenly winked on, and Bolan dived to the tarmac.

The triggerman was lining up a shot, but startled by the landing lights, he delayed his shot a half second. A resounding boom shattered the silence.

The warrior rolled over, thrusting the Desert Eagle in front of him.

The lights made it difficult to see, but at last he spotted the man. It was Steiner, his face a mask of fury.

A red laser spot traced a line across the tarmac. It was on Bolan's leg as he fired a quick shot in the direction of the German terrorist. With no time to aim, he had to count on rattling Steiner.

The Desert Eagle was good for that. Its roar and flash made a man know he was at the receiving end of overwhelming firepower. The big slug hit the ground in front of Steiner and a little to his right, kicking up an eruption of soil and grass.

The spot of intense red laser light shifted to Bolan's shoulder, moving toward his head.

But the warrior was quicker. The Desert Eagle roared again, and Kurt Steiner's head exploded.

10

Seeing no reason not to touch down, the pilot brought his sleek twin-engine Piper to a smooth landing on the little hilltop airport.

Beside the pilot was a lean, hard-muscled man named Ian Fitzgerald. He was delivering half a million dollars' worth of cocaine and expected to collect the cash before he took off.

Fitzgerald took no chances when the prize was this high. He carried a Browning Hi-Power automatic in a holster under his arm and a Heckler & Koch HK-94 assault rifle behind his seat. To be doubly sure nothing went wrong, his pilot—the only man Fitzgerald trusted—was an ex-con who carried a Beretta on his hip, and wasn't afraid to use it.

The pilot made his turn at the end of the runway and began to taxi back toward the hangar. Then something strange caught his eyes. He stared intently at the side of the runway.

"Jesus H. Christ!" the pilot shouted.

Fitzgerald spun around. "What is it?"

The color had drained from the pilot's face. He wore a mask of utter horror and was unable to speak.

What the pilot saw was the headless corpse of Kurt Steiner. What he didn't see was the black-clad figure of Mack Bolan crouched on the ramp, out of the runway lights.

"Steiner," Bolan said as McGraw joined him. "Make sure the deputy stays alert. They might have seen."

McGraw headed back toward the hangar.

The Piper came along slowly, engines throttled back so as to make as little noise as possible. Fitzgerald stared toward the ramp, looking for Keppler's men. Then he saw it, too.

"Holy shit."

The pilot needed no orders. He shoved in the throttles.

The deputy who'd been told to shoot out the airplane's tire didn't wait for orders, either—he fired. The tire burst, and the plane swung around crazily and stopped.

The pilot switched on the airplane's landing lights, which momentarily blinded Bolan.

In an instant, Fitzgerald was out on the right wing, aiming his Browning. But with the pilot rocking the plane with his retreat onto the left wing, and the propellers still turning, it was difficult for him to fix his aim.

Bolan squinted into the lights, trying to recover his sight, and he squeezed off a shot from the Desert Eagle. He missed the drug runners, but his slug bore into the nose of the plane and on through the cockpit.

Sheriff Eddy took out the pilot before he could get off a shot.

There was no getting out of there, and Fitzgerald knew it. Seized by an idea, he snatched the pilot's microphone out of its clip. He'd seen him switch on the runway lights by holding down the transmit key, and hoped holding it down again would turn them off again. He pressed the key and held it down. The runway lights went out.

Bolan advanced on the plane, as Fitzgerald retrieved the assault rifle from inside the cockpit. The warrior was blinded again and threw himself to the ground as Fitzgerald pulled the trigger several times in quick succession.

One of the shots ripped through Bolan's flesh, just below his ribs. The wound burned like fire, and the warrior could feel the warm stickiness of his blood under the blacksuit.

McGraw was up on his knees with his rifle, snapping off shots at the plane to no avail. Ian Fitzgerald was already running fast through the darkness beyond the runway toward the distant woods.

The firefight was over.

A deputy ran back to the sheriffs' cars and retrieved a first-aid kit.

The bullet had gone straight through four inches of Bolan's flesh without striking bone. The deputy poured antiseptic powder into the entry and exit wounds, then taped a huge gauze pad to Bolan's side.

"We'll take you to a doctor," Sheriff Eddy told him.

Bolan shook his head firmly. "Let me get on my feet."

They helped him stand. The Executioner meant to move before his body stiffened. He walked toward the hangar with the two sheriffs and a deputy.

The Piper's engines still ran, so the other deputy climbed aboard to shut them down. Inside the airplane, he found the cocaine packed in several plastic garbage bags. It was a huge supply.

Bolan and the lawmen arrived in the hangar to find one of the three handcuffed prisoners slumped on the floor, dead.

"What the hell's this?" Sheriff Eddy muttered. He drew his revolver and pressed it to the forehead of one of the survivors. "What happened?"

The prisoner shook his head. "I don't know. I swear I don't."

McGraw knew the other prisoner. He stood in front of him, his face inches away, looking hard and threatening. "What happened to him, Chuck?"

"He took poison," Chuck replied dully. "He had it in his pants pocket and managed to get it out on the floor where he could lap it up." He shook his head. "I hope I don't ever have to see a man die that way again."

A deputy found the money in a bag in the trunk of one of the cars. "Enough to make a man wonder if he's on the right side of the law," the deputy said somberly.

A DOCTOR WAS WAITING when McGraw returned Bolan to the farmhouse outside Marietta. He pronounced himself satisfied with the way the deputy had treated the wound, then numbed it and cleaned it out. After he had bound it with new bandages, he gave the warrior two injections.

"Sleep until sometime tomorrow afternoon," he said. "Then plan on staying in bed a few days. I'll come back to check on you in a couple days—sooner if need be."

"Got work to do," Bolan told him.

"Well, you aren't going to do any more in the next twelve hours," the doctor announced. "One of those shots was an antibiotic to fight infection. The other was a sedative. You'll sleep tight for twelve hours, big fellow."

WHEN BOLAN opened his eyes, brilliant daylight streamed through the bedroom window. Donna sat on a chair facing him, reading a paperback book.

Bolan swung his legs over the side of the bed and forced himself to stand. His body was still weak from the sedative and his side throbbed, but he managed to move around the room.

"What's happened since—"

"Plenty," she replied. "But you're not the only guy in the world who can take care of it. I'll tell Brad you're up. You can have food and a talk at the same time."

Five minutes later he sat in the kitchen. Donna handed him a cup of coffee, as Brad Updike began his briefing.

"We got fingerprints off the airplane," he stated. "The guy who shot you is named Ian Fitzgerald. Five years ago he escaped from a British prison, where he was serving a sentence for a bombing in Northern Ireland. IRA type. He managed to get into the U.S. and was arrested again in Boston. He skipped bail before the authorities there found out who he was. Two years later he's known around Chicago as a street dealer, then two years after that as a wholesaler. That's where the plane came from—Chicago."

"What about Johnson?" Bolan asked.

"He's gone. Checked out of the Lafayette Hotel this morning. By the way, his real name is Gerd Keppler. He does have an oil company in Texas, and he does use the name Johnson. We haven't been able to dig up any evidence of criminal activity, but the man has an amazing assortment of friends—everyone from drug dealers and terrorists to politicians and celebrities."

Bolan drained his coffee and sat for a minute trying to put the various pieces of the puzzle together. If Takahashi was recruiting the troops, Keppler must be the money and the connections behind the operation.

"Did you get a make on the guy who poisoned himself?" Bolan asked.

Updike nodded. "He couldn't afford to be held and identified. The name was Selko. He was a real celebrity on the terrorist circuit. The guy was wanted in twelve states, and God knows how many foreign governments would have found unpleasant ways of putting him to death."

"Are we any closer to getting where we're going?" Bolan asked.

"Depends on where you're going. You're supposed to go to Washington. Hal wants you in for a briefing."

"When?"

"Sleep some more on the plane," he said. "He wants you there tonight, if you'll go. He'll have a jet at the airport for you whenever we give the word."

THE WORD WENT BY RADIO to Washington. By the time Bolan had bathed and had been driven to the Wood County airport, they had only ten minutes to wait for the government Lear jet to arrive.

The Executioner arrived at the Justice Department early in the evening. Despite his protests he found himself hustled to an infirmary, where a doctor removed his bandages, examined his wounds, gave him another shot of antibiotics and bound him up again.

Half an hour later, Bolan was seated at a conference table.

"You've hit them hard, Striker," Hal Brognola began, "but we haven't stopped the main threat yet. The Green and Black is accumulating explosives, and one of these days the organization is going to be ready to make their move."

"Those explosives are on the river somewhere," Bolan said. "A wharf, or a barge. I'd guess a barge. Whatever, they're close to Marietta."

"Or maybe not," the big Fed stated. "Maybe they've centered everything else around Marietta to fool us. It's possible that the dam they want to take out is fifty or a hundred miles from there."

Bolan shrugged.

"Anyway, I've got some intel I want to go over with you. If you agree, I want to shift the focus. Your introduction to this problem was a trip on the river aboard the *Henry J. Muldoon*. The boat belongs to

Riverland Oil, as you remember. The captain is Doyle Tolliver.''

"I was impressed with the guy," Bolan said.

"So's Riverland Oil. Anyway, we might have gotten a much-needed break."

"I'm listening."

"The night you busted up the drug delivery, there was a guy who shouted a warning. We never found out who it was, but Captain Tolliver's convinced he's still got a bad guy on board."

"Meaning?"

"Meaning, it might well be the *Muldoon* that's going to blow up a lock."

"I still don't follow."

"Since you left, there's been some more incidents. A man fell overboard one night. Tolliver believes he was pushed. Then the next night, the *Muldoon*'s lead barge hit a skiff. Two Palestinians were fished out of the water by the Pennsylvania police."

"That's a guess. The river—"

"Has a thousand boats," the big Fed interrupted. "But this is the one we *know* has a rotten crew member. The *Muldoon* has made its turn now and is on the way back downstream. I want you to ride it down the river."

"That could put me in the wrong place."

"We can snatch you off in an hour if anything starts to go down somewhere else. Besides..."

"Besides what?"

"You got a hole in you, Striker. Coming down the river on the *Muldoon* won't be as athletic as some of what you've been doing."

The Executioner's eyes turned hard. Although Hal Brognola had been his friend for many years, what he was saying could never be accepted. The warrior had done his duty at times when he suffered far worse than this. He was a soldier first, and last. To stand on the sidelines for something that *might* be went against everything he believed in.

Brognola sensed some of his friend's thoughts.

"What I'm asking you to do is important! Dammit, Striker this isn't light duty. The fact is it's the best we've got to go on right now."

"Put like that, I can't say no."

Brognola grinned. "You never do. And counting on that, I've had the word put out in Marietta that you were flown out to be put in a hospital. You can figure that Fitzgerald has made contact with the Green and Black by now and probably told them that you're wounded. So it fits. You're out of the line for the time being for medical treatment. They'll buy it."

"Where do I board the *Muldoon*?"

"Pittsburg. Tomorrow morning. I'm putting an arsenal on board for you. Your cover is still the company cop, Belasko. As well, you'll see somebody you know on board. The two of you are to pretend that you don't know each other. You can watch and give intel to each other, through Captain Tolliver, and nobody's the wiser."

"Who?"

Brognola smiled. "You're gonna love it. Donna Dow."

Bolan shook his head. "Absolutely no," he said emphatically.

"Too late. She's on the *Muldoon* right now."

"Hal, you know how I feel about involving civilians."

"In the first place, she volunteered. She conned Updike into giving her some basic pointers while you were out working. She's smart, she's brave and she's the new assistant cook on the towboat. The story is that the company hired her for a boat's cook and she's learning the ropes from Lisa."

Bolan sat impassively. He didn't want to voice the thoughts that were going through his head.

"I knew you wouldn't like it," Brognola went on, "but she fits. She's from the river and knows it. There's nobody else who could work the cover. Her orders are to keep her eyes and ears open and don't try to be some kind of little tin heroine."

"Did you issue her a gun?" Bolan asked.

Brognola nodded. "She wouldn't go without it. Updike gave her a couple hours' instruction with it. Walther PPK. Small, but effective."

"Like she's supposed to be," Bolan said dryly. "Who's responsible when she gets herself killed?"

GERD KEPPLER WAS on Muskrat Island with Ian Fitzgerald. The Irishman had made his way to a highway, where he killed a young man and woman and took their car. Then he drove to Marietta, where he'd wakened Keppler to tell him that their shipment had been intercepted and that Keppler's men had probably been captured alive. The others might not know much, but Selko certainly did, and it was time for Keppler to pull out.

"So now Steiner," Takahashi said. "So be it. He was a reckless man and a fool. But Selko..." The Japanese shook his head. "He was a good man. And you two should know he'll never talk."

"You know him better than I," Keppler replied.

"Now," Takahashi said, "we have just about run out of sources of information. We have no one left in Marietta."

"I hear it was a dangerous town," Fitzgerald said.

"It contained one dangerous man," Takahashi answered. "I don't suppose Steiner accomplished his mission before he got himself killed?"

"I hit somebody," Fitzgerald said. "A big man with black hair. I saw him go down."

"Could it be?"

"It's possible," Takahashi said. He glanced at the Arabs still laboring at expanding the underground magazine, now nearly full with explosives. "In any case, that's what these men are to understand."

Fitzgerald settled an appreciative eye on Jasmin al-Said, who sat in front of her tent idly fingering the links of the chain that ran from her neck to the stake driven deep in the ground.

"Who is she?"

"She's a young woman who is to be left alone. If someone touches her, someone is dead."

"That is very plainly spoken," Fitzgerald said with a laugh. "Of course, I could take no interest in her, personally. She looks Muslim, and I'm a devout Christian."

Fitzgerald rose from the sandy soil and walked off toward the supply of liquor Takahashi kept in a crate in the entry to his own tent.

Once the Irishman was out of earshot, Keppler spoke quietly to the Japanese. "The *Henry J. Muldoon* leaves Pittsburg about noon tomorrow."

ONCE ON BOARD THE TOWBOAT, Donna realized that she'd signed on for a job of hard, sweaty work. The boat's cook, Lisa, was a good-hearted woman, but she was conscientious to a fault and wasn't satisfied unless food was available for "her boys" every hour of the day. She accepted the story that Donna was on the *Muldoon* to learn the tricks of the trade and was determined that she should learn everything—including her own painstaking devotion.

Skimpy clothing was out of the question with this crew of strong young men. Donna wore blue jeans—looser than she was accustomed to—and a light blue sweatshirt. The little Walther PPK was in a nylon holster just above her left hip. If a guy tried a feel, he'd find it. She was so determined that nobody would find it that the crewmen thought she was a little standoffish. Strange for a boat's cook, but so be it.

She was looking forward to Mike Belasko's arrival on board at noon tomorrow. In her kit she carried the antibiotics he was to take, plus fresh gauze pads to cover his wounds. Donna was determined to do her job well and to keep her ears open, but if for any reason he didn't show, she'd jump ship and to hell with it.

AT THE SAME TIME as Donna Dow slaved on board the *Muldoon*, Jasmin al-Said lay inside her tent watching the Japanese issuing orders to his men. In time he went inside his tent, leaving snoring guards in the clearing around the camp.

Jasmin tugged on her chain, which didn't clink. Night after night, when her captors were asleep, she'd learned to pull silently on the chain against the unyielding stake driven so deep in the ground. Finally the stake had begun to move a little. Then more. Tonight it moved several centimeters.

Maybe not tonight, but one night soon the stake would yield, and she'd pull it from the ground.

What would she do then?

11

Captain Doyle Tolliver idly rubbed a hand through his grizzled gray beard as he watched the big warrior walk across the gangplank and board the towboat. He noted that Belasko walked gingerly, and knew why. The Feds had trusted him with most of the story. Belasko wasn't a company cop, and they'd made a point that he wasn't a Fed, but he was to be treated as if he were.

"Mike! Good to see you!"

"Doyle. Good to see *you*."

It was, in fact, good to be back aboard the big diesel towboat. Bolan had developed a respect for life on the river during his previous stay on the vessel. The crew was made up of civilians, but the men worked with something of the discipline Mack Bolan experienced in the military.

But despite his feelings, Bolan had more important priorities. He believed Brognola's statement that weeding out the terrorist crewman was the best chance they had of stopping the Green and Black. The Executioner had a job to do, and the job always came first.

"I put you in the second officer's cabin," Captain Tolliver said. "Your, er, equipment is stowed there.

And Mike, the girl is aboard, bunking in with Lisa. But she'll be available whenever you want her."

Bolan grinned. "It's not that way, Doyle. She doesn't have to be available to me."

"My orders are to see to it that she is. She brought a medical kit with her, and she'll take care of you."

"I don't need taking care of."

"No? Well, I saw you walking up the gangplank. You're stiff, Mike, and you've got some pain. Don't play macho man with somebody who wants to help you."

Bolan grinned and extended his hand again to Doyle Tolliver. "Yes, sir, Captain."

The *Henry J. Muldoon* was moored on the south side of the Monongahela. At Pittsburg the Monongahela joined the Allegheny to form the Ohio River. The rivers were spanned by big bridges, which poured traffic into the downtown city.

Steel mills lay on both sides of the water, many of them idle. The mills had once lighted the night with the flames from their furnaces, but not for some years.

"We'll be pulling out shortly," Tolliver announced. "Nothing could possibly happen this afternoon. If you'll take my advice, you'll get some rest. After that, a man might need all his strength."

Bolan nodded. He'd been thinking the same and welcomed the opportunity both to examine the arsenal that Brognola had provided and to refamiliarize himself with the *Muldoon*. In addition to the twin bed, there was a desk and chair, a wash basin, a radio and a telephone. He opened the locker and found that his gear had in fact been delivered.

The centerpiece of his personal arsenal was a new machine pistol the Executioner had tested and learned to respect. The gun was called a Calico M-900, and it fired 9 mm rounds. Its unique feature was the helical magazine mounted on top of the weapon, which held one hundred rounds.

Hanging on the hooks in the locker were a black knit turtleneck shirt and black denim pants, and his black leather jump boots. The black nylon-webbing harness that carried his holsters, his knife, extra magazines for the Desert Eagle, and everything else that comprised the Executioner's combat outfit were there, as well.

As he examined his gear he heard the rumble of the diesels and felt the boat moving out into the river. Then there was a knock on the door. It was Donna.

"I'm supposed to check your temperature and your bandage," she announced.

He let her shove the thermometer into his mouth.

"I haven't seen or heard anything yet," she said. "There's a crew of about forty guys. Lisa says about half of them have been on the *Muldoon* for years, and the other half are guys that move from boat to boat, working part-time. I did hear one guy make a crack about the company cop being back aboard, but he's just a smart ass. I don't think he's trouble. Actually I haven't even seen all the crew yet."

She pulled the thermometer out. "You're normal."

"I could've told you that."

"Sure you could, but I wouldn't believe you. The big cheese in Washington, whoever he is, wants an honest, independent judgment on you."

"He sent you to spy on me."

"Something like that. What'd you think I'm on this tub for?"

"You'd better get back to the galley," he said. "You're not supposed to know me."

SEMTEX IS THE MOST powerful plastic explosive available anywhere. It is so powerful, in fact, that only a few ounces, molded into a radio, brought down the Pan Am flight over Lockerbie, Scotland, that killed 170 people. It's a favorite terrorist weapon.

It's also safe to handle. An orange-yellow substance, it's so odorless that it can't be detected by dogs trained to sniff out explosives, or by molecular sniffer machines. Fire won't set it off. Neither will any but the strongest shocks.

When the new Czech government halted the manufacture of Semtex, its price increased until it was worth twenty or thirty times what it had been before 1990. A terrorist who got his hands on some was considered something of an aristocrat in the profession.

It was for this reason that Keppler was smug about having used his contacts—plus a lot of cash—to obtain fifty kilograms of Semtex. He'd put up half the money in advance and was to pay the balance on delivery—tonight.

The explosives were aboard a handsome cabin cruiser that was coming upstream from Cincinnati. A little after sunset the cruiser passed through the lock at Belleville and entered the pool in the river that stretched past Marietta.

At the wheel of the cabin cruiser—called *Queen City Queen*—was its owner, a Kentuckian named Cooper. He used the cruiser to run untaxed liquor and narcotics on the river. In fact, for the right price anybody could use the *Queen City Queen* for whatever their purpose.

Relaxing below was such a man. He called himself David Benson and he was drinking white wine and nibbling on the foods that he'd insisted be aboard for his trip. Cooper knew what Benson was carrying in his huge attaché case.

He knew, and he didn't care.

After a while he identified Muskrat Island and turned the cabin cruiser toward the West Virginia shore. He'd been told to take this route because the river to the West Virginia side of the island ran along some farmland. It wasn't lighted at night, so they weren't likely to be seen.

Benson came up and stood beside him. "Is that Muskrat Island?"

Cooper nodded. "That's what the chart says."

"Switch off your lights," Benson instructed. "Show them for ten seconds every minute on the minute."

MACK BOLAN climbed back up to the pilothouse. His body was still stiff, and he felt pain when he moved abruptly, but he was rapidly regaining the strength that his wounds had sapped from him.

Captain Tolliver was steering the *Muldoon* through the short northerly course of the Ohio River called the Rust Belt. At one time it was a heartland for heavy industry, producing much of the nation's iron and steel. It had suffered deep depression of late years and was only just beginning to revive.

Bolan watched as the tow passed the cold and silent plants. He could see by the expression on the captain's face that he wanted to say something but was reluctant.

"Mike," he began uncertainly, "you know that I mean no disrespect, and that I'll help you in any way I can. But I don't believe there's any way they could use the *Henry J. Muldoon* to damage a lock. Hey, man, they'd have to take over the whole boat. If I got five crooks on board, I got thirty-five honest men."

"Armed?" Bolan asked.

"We got some weapons."

"You warned your men?"

"Well, no."

"Don't," Bolan said. "If you do you'd be warning the bad ones, which would only make things worse. Let's just watch. Let's watch and see what happens."

SAKO TAKAHASHI AND Gerd Keppler walked away from the little camp, into the woods and toward the West Virginia side of the island. The other men didn't notice. The Japanese worked them hard enough during the day that they ate and dropped exhausted as soon as the sun set.

Jasmin tugged on her chain. For four nights now, she'd been pulling, gradually loosing the stake in the sandy soil. The stake yielded more every time she tugged, and the princess thought that the time had come to take a chance.

She crawled toward the stake, as she had several times before, and scooped some sand around it to conceal the fact that it had been moving. Keeping an eye out to try to see if anyone watched, she approached the stake and warily reached out to touch it.

It *was* loose. She jerked it back and forth, but when she seized it with both hands and pulled upward, it wouldn't come.

She squatted beside it and jerked it back and forth again. The sand yielded, and the stake moved more and more.

Now she tried to lift it again.

It came, but grudgingly at first. For the first time that she could remember in a long time, Jasmin al-Said smiled. While it was too much to say that she was free, at least now she had a chance.

The stake was tapered, but the chain was padlocked to it so tightly that she couldn't take it off. As quietly as she could, she crawled away into the thorny brush toward the Ohio side of the river, carrying the heavy chain, and the stake, too.

The insects, thorns and nettles were relentless.

Her sweat-drenched skin was soon covered with scratches and bites, but she crawled on until she reached the river.

Gratefully she lowered her stinging body into the cool mud-brown water.

She wasn't a skillful swimmer at the best of times, and she knew that the chain was far more weight than she could carry in the water even for a short distance. To swim half a mile or more to the shore was impossible.

But she'd thought of this moment for days. She'd seen the river, and knew about the driftwood it carried after every rain. Some of it got stuck along the shores. Wading out into the water a few feet, Jasmin searched for a piece of wood big enough to help her.

Then she'd be free.

SAKO TAKAHASHI KNELT at the water line, knees in the sandy muddy, staring at the long expanse of moonlit river. He thought he'd seen the cruiser's red and green lights flash on and off.

"Forget the damned mosquitoes," he grunted to Keppler, "and watch for the damned lights."

"Why don't they bite you?" Keppler asked, at last voicing the question everyone had been afraid to ask.

"Question of will," Takahashi replied. "I *forbid* them to bite."

Keppler wished he hadn't asked.

Then the lights flashed on and off again. There was no question; the boat was out there.

"One more minute," Takahashi said.

When that minute elasped, the lights came on and Keppler returned the signal with a big flashlight.

The cabin cruiser edged up to the muddy shore. The man who called himself Benson—known by quite another name to Keppler—stood on the foredeck, briefcase in hand.

"Hello my friend," he said in German. "A beautiful night, isn't it?"

"Yes it is. But quick, quick, please."

Benson was a little put off by Keppler's nervousness. He'd noticed but taken no note of the nearly naked Oriental in the water beside the boat. As he handed down the briefcase with his right hand and reached for the money with his left, he dropped the briefcase and clutched his throat with both hands.

A blade had whipped into his throat, cutting through his windpipe and choking his breath. He staggered back and fell over the side of the boat, into the water.

Cooper saw, and immediately raised his hands. "Hey, guys! I didn't see anything. You guys do whatever you—"

Before the cabin cruiser owner could finish his sentence, he died the same way.

"Christ!" Keppler yelled at Takahashi. "That man represented ninety percent of the Semtex left in the world!"

Takahashi ignored him. "We load the boat with rocks," he said, "and sink it down there where the water is deep. And regarding this guy and all of the rest of them, none of them will mean anything when we—"

"You're crazy!"

"I'll pretend I never heard that."

Five minutes later, while striding back into the encampment after giving his orders for the sinking of the cabin cruiser, the Japanese found that Jasmin al-Said was missing.

He killed two of the encampment guards. Every other man on the island was sent to look for her.

JACK McGRAW PATROLLED a stretch of the river along West Virginia that, technically, was outside his jurisdiction. It didn't matter much. The West Virginia authorities were thankful for the Ohio sheriff's help, and no one was about to question his authority on the river, regardless of what county he came from.

McGraw used a small skiff powered by a small outboard. Knowing that it was better to sneak up on somebody rather than chase them, the skiff was dark and quiet. A deputy sat in the stern, steering. McGraw sat in front, staring at the moonlit water and at the dark banks of Muskrat Island.

At one time the island had been farmed, producing tons of truck crops—sweet corn, watermelons, cantaloupes and the like. People had lived their summers in vacation homes. It was hard to believe. Now the island was officially a wildlife preserve. Legally no one went ashore, except with a permit.

Moving quietly along the shore of the island, McGraw passed within twenty feet of the terrified Jasmin al-Said. The Qatari had been crouching in the willow thicket. She'd heard the insane rantings of the Japanese, his soldiers scurrying to find her, and was convinced they were in the boat now.

Directly above her, two men stood motionless in a stand of tall weeds, trying not to be seen by the men in the boat. They saw uniforms and knew they were lawmen. Very cautiously they moved back into the brush. Then they hurried back toward the camp to report.

BOLAN WAS FAIRLY CERTAIN that the big trouble waited down farther along the Ohio River and not where they were now. Even so, he made an armed recon of the tow before he went to his cabin and locked himself in for the night. Carrying the Beretta, nothing heavier, he walked around the *Muldoon*, then out onto the tow.

Having walked out to the lead barge, the Executioner stood as far as one could get from the rumbling diesels and listened to the water going under the barges. A big cloud was obscuring the moon, and other than the glow of the red and green running lights ahead and the dim outside lights on the *Henry J. Muldoon*, the barges were completely dark.

Suddenly he heard a loud clank of the steel deck, maybe five feet to his left. He stiffened and stared. Then he heard the slap of a rubber-soled shoe. He threw himself to the left and grabbed a vertical pipe.

The man in the sneakers drove himself forward like a football lineman throwing a block. His purpose was obvious enough. He meant to knock the company cop overboard. But Bolan had moved, so the man had thrown his block against empty air. He couldn't stop himself short of the edge of the barge and with a yell went over the side and fell to the water.

With more slip-slapping Bolan heard a second man, running in the dark. He stopped at the edge and looked down into the water.

"Hal?"

"Hal fell overboard," Bolan said coldly.

The man whipped around, pulling a pistol from his waistband as he turned. But the Executioner was ready. He fired one quick, muffled shot from the Beretta. The man staggered back and fell off the barge, a shot from his own pistol racing skyward.

In the galley, Bolan asked Donna where the captain was.

Tolliver was in his cabin, she'd said, the second pilot having come on duty. Donna went to the captain's cabin and woke him. Tolliver entered the galley a couple of minutes later, looking a little bewildered.

"You're short two men," Bolan said.

"*Somebody's* short two men," Tolliver replied.

"When you figure out who's missing, you might know something. Who were their friends? When did they come on board? One was called Hal."

Donna spoke. "Hal? He was in here drinking coffee fifteen minutes ago."

"Who with?"

She shrugged. "Another guy. I don't know their names yet."

"Two..." Tolliver mused. "I wish I could believe they were the only two bad ones I had aboard."

12

Ian Fitzgerald had spent hours listening to Takahashi and Keppler rant about the man who'd caused them so much troubled. He was sick of it, but he was troubled, as well. He'd begun to suspect something. It was just possible that the Green and Black leaders were worried about a man that Fitzgerald had met before, in Ireland.

Hadn't they called him the Executioner?

If that's who this guy was, then Fitzgerald wanted off the island, quickly. The scheme that Takahashi and Keppler had dreamed up, with all the riches that it promised, wouldn't do him any good if he was dead. And dead is what Fitzgerald was convinced he'd be if he had to face the Executioner.

The problem was that crazy Japanese bastard. Fitzgerald was convinced that he was insane. He'd seen what Takahashi had done to the two guards in his rage over losing the girl. The Irishman knew that the same fate was in store for himself, if he defied him.

Right now Takahashi sat cross-legged, rocking back and forth as if in some sort of meditative trance. What he was doing—Fitzgerald was certain—was plotting something wildly destructive.

IT WAS DARK NOW, and Jasmin al-Said cowered in the brush at the downstream end of Muskrat Island. Looking out at the wide expanse of water beyond the island, she was wet and cold. After spending the day carrying around ten feet of heavy chain, she was also tired.

She watched great diesel-powered towboats churning up or down the river, shoving long strings of big rusty barges. There were little boats with fishermen and turtle hunters, too. Hardly any of them approached Muskrat Island, but she'd have been afraid to hail a boat, in any case. So she crouched in the brush, and from time to time ventured into the water, to escape from the insects.

The night passed. When daylight came she wouldn't dare go into the water for fear of being spotted. It would be warm again. She'd sweat, and the mosquitoes would feast on her.

THE *HENRY J. MULDOON* moved downstream, making good time, working its way through locks and passing through the river's twisting channel.

"Think of the old boys who came down this river on flatboats or in dugout canoes," Doyle Tolliver said. He was a treasury of river lore and liked to talk about the old days when settlers loaded their families and their cattle on flatboats and braved a river that wasn't dammed.

It was a luxury to be able to focus one's mind on history—a luxury the Executioner couldn't afford. This morning, the warrior's thoughts were on what might happen in the next forty-eight hours.

Tolliver now knew who the two missing men were. Bolan had sent their names to Brognola, communicating by telephone and in code. The one called Hal was unknown to the law. The other man was an ex-con who'd done time for rape.

Donna brought hot coffee with pastries to the pilothouse and sat down to talk for a minute.

"There's a lot of talk in the galley about the two missing men," she said. "They'd worked on this boat for a month and had some friends."

"Has anybody figured out how they came to be missing?" Bolan asked.

She shook her head. "The idea seems to be that they jumped ship. The guys I've overheard figure they were involved in dealing dope and maybe took off with their profits."

"Watch the ones who don't have anything to say about it," Bolan suggested.

"Right," Tolliver agreed. "They're the ones who *know* what happened."

Bolan sensed that something was going to come down today or tonight. The *Henry J. Muldoon* would make it past Marietta and into the lower stretches of the river in the coming twenty-four hours. If this towboat was the target, then something had to happen soon.

What happened last night lent credibility to Brognola's theory. If this was the wrong boat, Bolan knew that nobody would bother to try to knock off the "company cop." They would have simply let him ride down the river, dumb and happy.

So, if the *Muldoon* had something to do with what the Green and Black were planning, the question was how to smoke them out.

One tactic that Bolan had employed successfully many times was to tempt the bad guys to try to take him out. Guys involved in schemes like this got nervous and impatient. The point was to lead them into making a stupid move.

He went down to his cabin, then below into the main cabin of the towboat. Then he sauntered through the galley, where three men sat at the table, eating and talking.

They didn't look up as he walked through. Bolan wasn't surprised. They thought he was a company cop, and even men who had nothing to hide didn't welcome the idea of a cop on board their boat. Rivermen thought of their boat as a sort of home, the crew as family. So regardless of why he was on board, a company cop was an intruder.

Having given everybody in the galley enough time to see that he remained alive and well, Bolan went back up on deck and walked toward the stern. He was conscious that at any time, a man could throw his weight through any door and knock him overboard. The warrior was alert, more alert than anyone could have guessed.

On the stern he stood and watched the wake. The big propellers churned up mud from the bottom, making the wake brown and white. Water was sucked under each side of the boat, then spun through the propellers and driven out behind. Bolan understood that the propellers ran inside heavy steel cages that kept out driftwood and debris. A man who fell overboard wouldn't be chopped by the blades. Held by their suction, he'd drown.

A riverboat was a hazardous place to work.

Bolan walked inside the engine room, where the great diesels rumbled and turned the propeller shafts. The room was clean and smelled of oil. The boat's engineer sat in an office chair and kept an eye on his gauges. He had before him a log in which he wrote entries from time to time. Two other men patrolled the engine room, one of them carrying a rag to pick up spots of oil.

The engineer looked up and nodded at Bolan, friendly enough.

Bolan nodded back and walked through to the other side of the engine room. He came to the door of a big storage room, filled with great wooden spools of wire cable, drums of lubricating oil and crates of spare parts.

The Executioner walked in, and they made their move.

The sliding door behind him closed, and he turned to see a man facing him with an automatic in his hand. The opposite sliding door closed, too, and a man stood with legs apart, brandishing a knife.

Bolan was caught between them.

The one with the pistol grinned and nodded. "Wasn't so hard to get you, smart guy," he sneered. "The first thing I want to know is who the hell you are."

"Who do you think I am?" Bolan asked.

The gunner shook his head. "That kind of answer isn't gonna do. If I have to persuade you, I'll have Manny take a few slices out of you."

Bolan glanced at Manny. He was a hard-looking man, and it appeared as though he couldn't wait to do some slashing with the knife he was waving. "Just give me the word, Howie."

"Manny and Howie." Bolan laughed. It was a good idea to get a pair like this mad. In fact, his only chance was for them to do something stupid. "The two stooges."

Howie was a thin, wire-muscled man, tense and apparently agile. Bolan judged him far more dangerous than Manny, even without the pistol. Bolan's taunt had irritated him, but he wasn't angry.

The warrior was wearing a nylon jacket to cover the leather holster that carried his Beretta. It was the only weapon he carried. With Howie's gun aimed at his chest, Bolan couldn't reach for the Beretta.

He had to wait for them to make a mistake.

"Last chance," Howie said. "Tell us what important stuff you have to do, and we might change our minds. Otherwise, you're going for a long swim."

"My name is Mike Belasko. I'm a company security man. Some people think that drugs are being hauled on this boat. I'm supposed to find out."

"If we believed that, we wouldn't have arranged this little party for you," Howie growled. "Try again, fella."

Bolan shrugged.

If he couldn't make Howie mad, maybe he could make him nervous. He started moving his right hand slowly up toward the Beretta.

"Uh-oh," Howie said with mock fear. "The guy's packin' heat. Step over here Manny and grab his piece. But be careful."

The chance Bolan was waiting for finally arrived.

Although Howie kept the pistol pointed at Bolan, Manny stepped halfway between and blocked him from firing. The knife was in Manny's right hand, with the point only an inch or two from Bolan's abdomen. He reached with his left hand for the Beretta, and while searching inside Bolan's jacket for the pistol, he momentarily forgot about his own weapon. It was all the time that the Executioner needed. Bolan grabbed the hand holding the knife and shoved it away.

Then he swung his body to the left, throwing his right foot in front of the hardman. In an instant Bolan's right arm was up and over Manny's neck. Then he threw him over his hip and heavily onto Howie—a classic Judo move.

Both men went down. Bolan jumped one heel down hard on Howie's right wrist, then the other on his elbow. Having broken the pistolman's wrist, the warrior kicked the weapon away.

Manny came up slashing. Thrusting forward, he threw himself off balance when Bolan stepped aside. The warrior drove a fist into his ear.

Howie scrambled across the floor toward his pistol, but Bolan grabbed him by the seat of the pants and threw him aside. As he sprang back to his feet and charged, he met a fist in the jaw and fell back.

Manny ran out the door and onto the deck, with Bolan in rapid pursuit. Before he could catch him, Manny jumped up on the rail and threw himself into a dive. Throwing himself far enough away from the hull of the *Muldoon* to escape the suction of the propellers, he hit the water flat and swam hard. In a moment he was ten yards from the towboat.

Howie came out with the pistol in his hand. Bolan dropped into a crouch and pulled the Beretta. Before either of them fired, they were startled by two sharp cracks from a door just ahead of them, followed by a shriek from the river.

Howie glanced back for an instant. When his eyes returned to Bolan, he found himself staring into the muzzle of the Beretta, with the Executioner crouched and poised to fire. Howie dropped his weapon and raised his hands in the air.

As Bolan approached, the disarmed thug suddenly threw himself overboard.

He dropped directly down the hull and disappeared under the towboat.

Bolan stared, disbelieving. The man had killed himself.

Beretta in hand, he searched the water for Manny. He was gone. The two shots from the door had found their mark.

Bolan eased forward along the bulkhead. He suspected that whoever had fired the shots would already be gone, but not so. Donna was there, inside the boat's big pantry. As Bolan slid around the door frame, she was already busy shoving her Walther back into its holster.

Her eyes were brittle, flashing. It was apparent that the gravity of killing a man had hit her. She looked at him, silent for a moment, then said, "They tried to kill you."

He nodded. There was no point in telling her she'd shot a man he'd wanted to question.

Donna fell into his arms and began to sob.

"You did the right thing," Bolan said. "Forget what just happened. It'll all be over soon."

THREE TIMES THEY'D COME to the very edge of the water, and three times Jasmin had slipped under with only her face above the surface.

Now she huddled in the mud and thought about food. She drank a little river water, afraid of what biology it might carry but too thirsty to resist it.

A little above her on the bank, a shrub was festooned with dark-red berries. She tasted a few, but they were bitter, and she was afraid they were poisonous. She spit them out.

Hungry, tired and afraid, Jasmin sat in the mud at the edge of the water and wept. She cried for her past mistakes and for the hopelessness of her present situation.

And, weeping, she failed to notice the little johnboat that came along the shore.

Dipping his oars gently, quietly watching the birds, Hank Mendenhall missed very little on the banks of the river. So far this morning he'd found a couple of pretty good planks washed up in the mud. Dried, and with the nails pulled, they'd be good for something.

Hank was fourteen years old, and some thought he wasn't too bright. But he'd found a lot of good stuff in the river. The johnboat he was in right now was an example. Nobody had claimed it, and it was a lot better than the one he'd used before.

Looking toward the riverbank Hank couldn't believe what he saw. A beautiful girl was sitting asleep—or looking like she was asleep—with her head on her drawn-up knees. But something was wrong. The girl was smeared with mud and swollen with bites. Then he noticed the chain fastened around her neck with a lock, and wrapped around her body.

Hank nosed the johnboat to shore not five feet from her. He was quiet, but it startled her. She jumped to her feet and drew back like an animal about to be hit with a club.

"Don't worry. I ain't gonna hurt you."

Jasmin knew instantly that he wasn't one of them. He was too young. He stared at her with a childish, innocent look. Even if he had been one of them, she knew she couldn't have escaped.

"Do you need help?" he asked.

Jasmin nodded. "They... want to kill me," she muttered hoarsely.

"Who wants to kill you?"

She glanced back over her shoulder. "Bad men. Dangerous men."

Rescuing a beautiful girl in trouble was like a dream come true for Hank. He pointed at the bow of his boat and told her to get in.

She looked back toward the woods. "If they see—"

Gesturing at her to lie down in the boat, he threw a jacket over her. Then, seeing that it didn't cover her well enough, he took off his shirt and put that over her, too. Finally he laid his two planks on top of her, and she was hidden.

With one oar, Hank shoved his johnboat out into the current. He grabbed up a cane pole and threw a line overboard. No one would notice that his hook wasn't baited. He sat hunched over as if he were fishing, keeping one eye on Muskrat Island. The current carried the johnboat steadily downstream. He waited until he was almost a mile from the island before he pulled his line in and bent his back to the oars.

It wasn't until much later that Jasmin al-Said poked her head up and knew she was free.

"SOMETHING IS coming down," Fitzgerald said to Keppler, "and damned soon. So, if I'm going to fight, I'd like to know what the fight is about."

Keppler glanced at Takahashi, who was now in the bunker, working hard and streaming sweat.

"He's rigging the biggest bomb that's ever been seen in this part of the country," Keppler replied. "And in spite of everything that's happened, we're ready to do what we came here to do."

"Which is?"

The German glanced again at the laboring Japanese. "What do you like? The freedom of the oppressed, or enough money to live like a goddam

Oriental potentate for the rest of your life? Which is your cause?''

Fitzgerald grinned. ''The oppressed have always been a special concern of mine,'' he said sarcastically.

''We'll make a share for you, when we win,'' Keppler said easily. ''I have no doubt that Takahashi will go along with that, depending on your contribution.''

''Contribution to what?'' Fitzgerald asked. ''I don't see competence at its highest here.''

''Sideshows. We've been beaten on the sideshows. Tonight we make the world sit up and take notice. Down the river a few miles is Belleville lock and dam,'' Keppler continued. ''We're going to put a barge loaded with explosives in the lock and detonate it. Boat and barge traffic on the Ohio River will be interrupted for six months at the very least, costing the United States government and industry billions. I mean billions. We've asked for a big ransom not to do it, but they haven't paid. So we're going to show them. Then if they don't pay, we'll do it again.''

Fitzgerald shrugged. ''What I see is tons of explosives in a bunker. How does it get into the lock?''

''In a barge,'' said Keppler, who glanced at his watch. ''At dusk a barge will be pushed up to this island. Our men will load it with the explosives, and the barge will be shoved out into the channel. Tonight the little boat pushing that one barge will rendezvous with a big towboat pushing a dozen barges. Our barge will be added to the tow. When the tow enters the Belleville lock—''

"Boom," Fitzgerald said skeptically. "How is this big towboat going to be persuaded to take this floating bomb into its care?"

"We've got a dozen men in its crew," Keppler replied. "Others will come aboard and complete the takeover."

Fitzgerald watched the near-naked Takahashi herding his men here and there, himself working like a slave. "You've got there a man who's more interested in the boom he's going to make than the money he's going to get out of it."

"He's my partner," Keppler said quietly. "Suppose soon there were just two partners...and Sako Takahashi wasn't one of them?"

Fitzgerald smiled cynically. "I wonder how that might come to pass."

CAPTAIN DOYLE TOLLIVER handed a special scrambled telephone to Bolan. They were in the pilothouse.

"Brad Updike has Jasmin al-Said at the farmhouse," Brognola said.

"We've now confirmed that the Green and Black have tons of explosives in a bunker on the first island downstream from Marietta. Muskrat Island."

"Who's there?" Bolan asked.

"Sako Takahashi. From the description al-Said gives, I'd say your German friend, as well. They're still plotting the big blast."

"Where?"

"It's gotta be a dam."

"I'm—" the warrior turned to Tolliver, who put a finger on a chart "—fifty miles upstream. You were right. This boat is part of the plot."

"What do you want me to do?" The big Fed asked.

"Notify Jack McGraw and tell him to keep his distance. I want to clean this thing up all at once, and this isn't the kind of thing a small-town sheriff can handle—no matter how brave he is."

"You got it," Brognola replied. "You're the head man. Don't let the bastards get the jump on you."

13

The *Henry J. Muldoon* could have covered the fifty miles to Muskrat Island in a few hours, but there were four dams between the towboat and Marietta. That meant the tow had to be disassembled four times, once for each lock. It would be dark by the time they locked through at Dam 17 and entered the river pool where Muskrat Island lay.

While the *Muldoon* was still several hours away, a sand-and-gravel boat much like the *Sterling Bradbury* busily pushed its one barge through the narrow channel between Muskrat Island and the West Virginia shore. If a towboat like the *Muldoon* had gone that way, it would have caused notice, even excitement, along the river. For a little sand-and-gravel boat to do it was nothing special.

The boat passed the tip of the island, where two sentries stood watch. One turned and ran toward the encampment through more than a mile of woods choked with briars and nettles, to give the word.

He reached the camp as Keppler and Takahashi were issuing weapons. Every man on the island—there were still more than twenty of them—would have an Uzi carbine and some kind of side arm. Men who'd done sentry duty these past weeks had already been issued weapons. The men who received them tonight were the laborers who'd sweated to dig out the bunker. Some of them had begun to wonder if they weren't just slaves, only to be murdered when their work was done. They accepted their weapons with grim satisfaction. With guns in their hands, they knew they were fighters once again.

Half a dozen men were on sentry duty at points around the island. Takahashi gathered the rest. The crew was a motley assemblage, including wrathful Arabs with a burning hatred for America, two Japanese who were committed to this business strictly for the profit they expected from it and some Americans. The Americans were the worst sort of scum the country produced: escaped convicts; ex-cons with records that included rape, child abuse, murder and robbery; a deserter from the Marine Corps; plus a student "revolutionary" who was wanted for firebombing a university laboratory building.

They had little in common except their awe of—their *fear* of—the nearly naked man who spoke to them. Besides his loin cloth, tonight he wore a strip of white cloth around his head that was lettered with black Japanese characters. He spoke in the strained voice of a fanatic, shouting out his words to listeners who were no more than a few yards from him.

"In an hour we'll be gone from this hellish place. None of us will stay. Some will go on the towboat or barge, the rest in smaller boats.

"We'll load the explosives as soon as the barge arrives. Then the little towboat will move the barge to the dock across the river, on the Ohio side. The big

towboat coming down the river will have been taken
over by our comrades well before it arrives here. All of
us will board the big towboat and ride it downstream.
When the lead barges are in the lock at Belleville, we'll
abandon the towboat and go ashore. The barges in the
lock will then be lowered to the level of the downstream pool, and we'll detonate the explosives. The
river will roar through the lock, carrying the towboat
and barges, completing the devastation.''

AT THE SAME TIME as Sako Takahashi was harangu-
ing his troops, the *Henry J. Muldoon* entered the lock
at Willow Island, the second one upstream from
Marietta.

Bolan had decided to ride one of the lead barges
through the lock. He wanted to familiarize himself
with the procedure on the chance that his business with
the Green and Black wasn't finished at Muskrat Island. Understanding their plans could be the last advantage the Executioner had if things didn't go well.

Captain Tolliver eased the first eight barges into the
lock. Deckhands ran back and forth, looping heavy
rope over cleats on the lock wall. At the break of the
four barges closest to the *Muldoon,* crewmen loos-
ened the tension off wire cables, preparing to free
them.

Once the separation was complete, Tolliver backed
the towboat away from the upstream gates, and they
began to close. Big valves were opened and the water
ran out of the lock. The water level began to drop, and
the barges began to descend, bumping against con-

crete walls with enough force to crush anything that came between them.

Bolan heard nothing, saw nothing, but he felt the knife hit his back. He spun around, but he couldn't tell which man had thrown it. Nobody showed a sign of seeing the attack.

No one even showed a sign of being startled to see the company cop standing there glaring at them with a knife sticking in his back, in one of the solid nylon plates of the body armor he'd decided he'd better wear tonight. He hadn't yet changed into his combat suit, but he saw no reason to think he wouldn't be attacked again.

He reached behind and pulled the knife out. It was a balanced throwing knife, with two blades, no handle—a weapon a man could learn to use without too much practice. He'd been standing three feet back from the edge of the barge. If the knife hadn't hit body armor, he would very likely have stumbled forward and down into the gap between the barge and the lock wall.

He tossed the knife overboard, favored the staring men with a sour little smile and walked back along the barges.

As far as Jack McGraw was concerned, the animals that had wreaked havoc on his town had to be stopped, whether Muskrat Island was in his jurisdiction or not. That hadn't been easy to explain to the Justice Department, but that's the way it was. He also owed one to Mike Belasko, and he'd be damned if he left the big warrior to battle alone.

McGraw and two deputies were now on the river in a fast boat powered by a big outboard. The sheriff of Wood County, West Virginia, was on the river with deputies in another boat, and two other boats with West Virginia State Police officers cruised around the island.

All of the lawmen were armed with heavy police weapons—rifles and short-barreled shotguns. None of them was armed with automatic weapons, such as Uzis.

Two of the boats met in the middle of the channel between the island and the West Virginia shore. Jack McGraw was in one, Lieutenant Davis from the West Virginia State Police in the other.

"You want to go ashore?" Davis asked.

In the last purple light of the sunset, McGraw scanned the wooded shore of the island. "If what the girl said is true, we could get caught in one hell of a trap," he said. "Fanatics with automatic weapons."

"We'll never find out if we don't go ashore," the lieutenant replied.

"I disagree. I say we sit tight and wait for them to make a move."

In essence, that was the compromise he'd reached with the Feds. The Green and Black was going to have to make its move by carrying its explosives off the island. Rather than charging in, McGraw had accepted the wisdom of trying to intercept the terrorists.

"Doesn't bother me," Davis said.

McGraw nodded. "Hey... What's that coming?"

He'd spotted a small towboat that was pushing the one barge, edging toward the island side of the channel.

"Let's have a look at her," Davis suggested. "Down the other side, not the island side."

A few minutes later the towboat's pilot was trying to explain to the West Virginia State Police that he was on his way home and had come up the West Virginia side of Muskrat Island to avoid traffic.

"Where's home?" Davis asked coldly.

"Well, it's Point Pleasant, usually. But tonight I'm tying up at Ben's Run, so's to be able to get a good start in the morning on a load of gravel I'm pickin' up."

Lieutenant Davis didn't guess that he was in the sights of two Uzis, ready to fire. The men who held those muzzles on him listened to the talk and looked around, scanning the situation. There were too many boats on the river. A burst of fire taking down a cop would bring heavy reinforcements.

"Keep moving, then," Davis said. "Stay away from the island over there. That's a wildlife refuge."

The pilot nodded. Scared and miserable he pointed his boat and his one barge for the middle of the channel and on up the river.

SAKO TAKAHASHI STOOD in the cover of the brush and watched the little towboat pass beyond the head of the island out of sight. His fury was beyond limit. Glancing around at the men who had to obey him, he smiled bitterly and said, "We'll transfer our explosives directly from the island to the *Muldoon*'s barges. It will be ours when it passes here anyway, so we'll carry our material out in our boats and load it on one of the big gasoline barges. Even if we don't get every last kilo of it aboard, we'll load enough to do the job!''

Keppler and Fitzgerald stood staring at him, confused and amazed.

"There's work to do!" Takahashi screamed. "All boats will have to be carried over to the Ohio side so those fools out there don't see us moving them around! We must hack a path through the brush. When the *Henry J. Muldoon* arrives, we'll be ready!''

AFTER TOLLIVER'S TOWBOAT passed through the last lock above Marietta, the captain reassembled the tow and pushed out into the channel. The sky was black now.

And Mack Bolan was wearing black. In his cabin, Donna had watched him change into the black clothes and strap himself into the harness that changed the big warrior into the ominous night figure of the Executioner.

"Go up in the pilothouse with Captain Tolliver," he said, "and stay there. I don't want either of you coming down. Things might start to happen quickly, and you can help me most by not trying to help me."

"Lisa will want me in the galley."

"The pretense is over. You'll be leaving the boat tonight, no matter what."

He climbed the gangways to the pilothouse with her.

"Good God!" Captain Tolliver exclaimed as he saw the man in black carrying the Calico M-900 machine pistol.

"He wants us to stay up here and out of the way," Donna told the captain.

Tolliver fingered his grizzly beard. "It's the best thing we can do," he said. "But I've got a thing or two ready, just in case."

He nodded toward the bench behind the wheel. A Colt .45 and a pump-action shotgun with very little barrel lay there.

Bolan shook his head. "Lock the door and stay in here behind your bulletproof glass. The most important thing is that you control the boat."

"You got it."

The warrior turned to leave the pilothouse. He stopped at the door and asked a question. "Are you expecting any mail boats or any other legitimate boats?"

"Not between here and Parkersburg," Tolliver replied.

"Then any boat coming alongside is—"

"Hostile," Tolliver finished the sentence.

BRAD UPDIKE'S ORDERS were to stay put at his communications center until further notice. He had six men, armed with M-16s, ready to move when ordered.

He had already put Jasmin al-Said aboard a federal jet that transferred her to a hospital in Washington. The Qatari girl was in a sorry state, as much with guilt for her misguided collaboration with the drug runners as from the shock of her ordeal on Muskrat Island.

The astonished Hank Mendenhall had been promised a reward and threatened with federal prison if he spoke a word about her.

Updike had been in the service of the Justice Department for three years. He'd heard rumors about a man who had carte blanche from the White House. He believed that he'd met him as "Mike Belasko."

If the big warrior was who he thought he was, Updike was confident that he could be counted on.

TWO STREAMS ENTER the Ohio River just above Marietta. One is called Duck Creek, the other Little Muskingum River. Four outboard-powered skiffs waited, out of sight, in the Little Muskingum, under the bridge that carried Ohio Route 7. A man with binoculars scanned the river. He knew the *Muldoon* had passed through Lock 7, so it had to be in sight.

It was.

He scrambled down the bank and used his flashlight to signal the skiffs a few yards back under the bridge.

Aboard the *Henry J. Muldoon*, a man employed under the name of Joe Calvin was disturbed that he didn't know where the company cop was. That was potentially dangerous, considering how many murder attempts the man had survived. But Calvin was confident that the big man's luck was now running out.

He checked his Uzi, which he carried openly now—and God have mercy on the boat's officer who objected. Although he passed easily as an American, Calvin's real name was Saladin. He'd fought with Uzis and had fought with more up-to-date weapons. At least this weapon felt comfortable and familiar in his hands.

The skiffs were coming out of the Little Muskingum. Saladin knew they'd come alongside the tow, and the six surviving fighters of the Green and Black would be supplemented by a dozen more.

The point now was to take control of the boat.

Saladin raised a hand to signal another *Muldoon* crewman. Morris knew what the signal meant. He stepped out from just below the pilothouse, pulled the pin on a grenade and threw it with all his force at the glass door of the pilothouse.

It was supposed to kill the pilot, but the Green and Black were unaware of the *Muldoon*'s bullet-proof glass. The grenade bounced off the glass and fell back toward Morris.

He screamed as it detonated, all but cutting him in two.

Bolan saw and heard the explosion from out on the barges. Expecting something like this, he'd told Tolliver to cut the lights on the outside of the *Muldoon* and on the barges. In the dark, the black-clad Executioner watched the outboard-powered skiffs come alongside.

He knelt beside a tangle of pipes and valves on the deck of the gasoline barge.

A rope came up first, looping over a cleat on the barge. The first invader climbed aboard, cradling an Uzi and looking around in the dark for anyone who dared to oppose him.

A moment later, a second man climbed on the barge. He was a fool. He switched on a big flashlight and began to search the barge. Bolan took him out with the Beretta. A subsonic round from the sound-suppressed pistol punched through the chest of the river pirate, and he fell back into the skiff.

The man with the Uzi set himself to fire, but the Beretta's flash-suppressed round gave him no target. He took Bolan's second shot in the throat and dropped into the river.

The gunmen in the other skiffs saw their fellow gang members go down. They stood in their boats and opened fire on the barge, sweeping its deck with a deadly storm of 9 mm stingers.

Slugs spranged off the deck, inching closer to Bolan. But the Executioner had his target and opened fire with the Calico subgun.

Bolan didn't fire at random like the gunmen, who hoped to hit their man simply by sweeping the whole barge with fire. They might have succeeded, if they'd coordinated themselves. But that kind of discipline was too much to expect of this kind of men.

Bolan turned his weapon on the nearest of the skiffs and fired three short bursts at the blue-yellow muzzle-flashes of the Uzis. The boat went silent as he ducked among the deck pipes and ran back toward the *Muldoon*.

Saladin had heard the shooting up front and understood that his forces were engaged. This only compounded his frustration at not getting into the pilothouse quickly and taking command of the boat. He now had to wonder if Captain Tolliver was up there on the radio, calling for help.

Saladin couldn't let that happen. Dashing up the gangway, he leaped out on the upper deck behind the pilothouse and fired bursts into the antenna control boxes. Within a minute he'd shattered them all. While he was at it, he shot out the searchlights, which also could have been used for signaling.

In the meantime, the leader of one of the skiffs out of Bolan's line of fire had ordered his men to concentrate their fire on the pilothouse. The impenetrability of the bullet-proof glass reached its limit, as the pressure of hundreds of slugs broke the glass.

Bolan raced toward the hostile skiff as Tolliver snatched up his pump-action shotgun, taking out one of the gunmen. The warrior took out two more with a burst from his subgun.

Bolan continued running toward the towboat and leaped from the last barge to the deck of the *Henry J. Muldoon*. A man jumped out from the shelter of the main cabin and snapped off a single shot at him. It whizzed past Bolan's ear, and the gunner was gone before the warrior could send a reply.

Then Bolan heard Saladin on the roof of the main cabin, which was below the pilothouse. He was yelling at the men in the skiffs to watch for the man in black. Since his position posed no immediate threat to either Tolliver or Dow, Bolan ran back along the side of the towboat. The biggest threat right now was still the incoming skiffs, and the Executioner meant to intercept them as they appeared.

The *Muldoon* was still moving downriver at normal speed. At least a score of men cowered in their cabins, terrified by the heavy gunfire on the decks of the boat that they thought of as their home away from home.

Bolan circled the rear of the engine room and ran out to the West Virginia side of the *Muldoon*.

One of the skiffs had come alongside and was already lashed to the towboat. By the time two of its gunmen climbed over the side and onto the vessel, Bolan had come through the storage room where Howie and Manny had tried to kill him that morning. Bolan used the silenced Beretta to drop the two gunmen before they knew what hit them.

Then, two thundering booms from the pilothouse blew that skiff full of shot.

Nearly blind with fury, Saladin screamed at anyone who could hear him. "Take the pilot out! Use your goddam grenades!" he yelled.

Not realizing that both Tolliver and Bolan could hear, two men ran out onto the lower deck with grenades in their hands. Bolan hit one in the face as he leaned back to toss the grenade through the shattered pilothouse window. The man fell back into the water, followed by the grenade, which exploded, throwing up a geyser of river water.

The second man was on the lower front deck, out of Bolan's sight. Tolliver blasted at him with the shotgun, and Donna fired three quick shots from her Walther PPK. It was difficult to tell which one got him, but he fell back, and his grenade exploded on the deck, blowing his body in the air.

The *Muldoon* moved quickly enough downstream that the skiffs didn't easily keep up. Two were out of the battle, one with nobody aboard but dead men.

One was following, while two men attended its other wounded men, and one hadn't yet moved in and taken its chances.

Bolan moved back through the storage room to the West Virginia side of the towboat. The man who had fired at him from the forward corner had to be there somewhere. He also knew someone could still be on the roof, moving along the side of the boat without being seen.

And he was correct. Saladin hadn't moved since shouting orders. He saw the big warrior moving beneath him and leaned over to throw a grenade under the roof overhang. It landed on the deck only six feet from where Bolan stood.

The Executioner shattered a window with the butt of his weapon and threw himself into the galley. The grenade exploded harmlessly as he fired a burst through the ceiling of the galley.

It caught Saladin in the left ankle, shattering the bone and leaving him in excruciating pain. He rolled toward the stern and out of the range, just before a second burst blasted through.

Bolan heard him scream but knew that the man who had fired from the corner was still around somewhere. He moved into the galley's pantry where he saw Lisa, the ship's cook, cowering among a shelf of provisions.

"Stay here and don't move," he ordered.

Lisa nodded, unable to speak.

As he stepped into the pantry's doorway, Bolan saw a fourth skiff moving alongside the towboat. In an instant, he leveled the muzzle of his weapon and opened fire. He was joined by Captain Tolliver and Donna Dow. Between the three of them, the men in the skiff didn't have a chance.

It was then that Saladin made a decision. He wasn't going to take the *Muldoon*. He'd been defeated.

Now he was left with two equally unappealing options. He could try to escape, or he could do whatever he could to take out the black-clad warrior. Even with his crippling injury, he made his decision without much difficulty. "Drake!" he yelled.

Drake was the man at the corner, who had been crouching with his Uzi ready, ever since he'd failed to kill Bolan on his first try. He had nothing much at risk. Convicts killed men like him in penitentiaries. So he couldn't go back. He'd kill Saladin as readily as the guy in black. The only difference was that Saladin had promised money and the guy in black hadn't.

"He's in the galley," Saladin yelled to him. "I'll come from up here, you from down there. Let's take him!"

Bolan wasn't in the galley; he was in the pantry. Although he didn't hear Saladin's instructions, he knew there was still at least one gunner loose. If they tried to take him out just by blowing the pantry apart, Lisa was dead.

This was when the M-900 proved more useful than any other automatic weapon he might have used. Having fired in short, controlled bursts, Bolan had spent maybe twenty rounds out of his 100-round magazine. He raised the muzzle and let the roof have four bursts. He still had rounds to spare.

Saladin tried to roll away from the explosions that came through the floor beneath him. He failed to roll far enough, or fast enough, to avoid the vicious fire coming up from below. He was hit again, this time in the hip.

Escape was no longer an option. Bleeding from both hits, Saladin tried to rise, failed, tried again, and lowered his Uzi to fire through whatever was under him.

A single stinging shot that severed his spinal cord put an end forever to any purposeful action by the man called Saladin. It was fired by Donna Dow.

Drake saw what had happened and understood. To hell with Saladin and Takahashi. To hell with the whole deal. He dropped his weapon and threw himself overboard, into the brown water of the Ohio River. He meant to swim away. He hadn't realized what the propellers would do.

14

Two boats emerged from the Ohio shore as the *Henry J. Muldoon* passed Marietta. They carried Brad Updike and a team of eight other federal officers, all armed with M-16s and dressed in camouflage fatigues. They brought a set of radios with them, so they could communicate with the sheriff and the police officers in still more boats on the river.

The regular crew of the *Muldoon* was back at work. They'd identified for Bolan the members of the Green and Black who'd chosen to throw their weapons overboard, rather than risk themselves against the "company cop" who had so soundly defeated Saladin's forces. They sat in a small cluster on the front deck, under the guard of the boat's engineer, who kept the captain's shotgun aimed at them.

Bolan got on the radio to Jack McGraw. "I think they'll come out and check us," he said. "That's the only way they're going to find out if their guys succeeded in taking over the boat."

"We're keeping a distance," McGraw told him. "If what Jasmin told us is true, there's a hell of a force on the island. Armed with heavy stuff."

"If they send a boat out, don't stop. That goes for the West Virginia guys, as well."

"Will do."

Captain Tolliver listened to this conversation, then touched Bolan on the arm.

"I've got an order," he said. "It came in by company radio before the shit hit the fan back there. I'm supposed to stop at a dock about a mile down and pick up an empty barge."

"Is that an unusual order?" Bolan asked.

Tolliver shrugged. "Sort of. The company's got a few barges that aren't tankers, or it could be somebody else's barge. Once in a while we move a barge for another company. I'd have got on the radio and asked for confirmation, but hell, they shot up all our radios."

"That barge could be loaded with explosives," Bolan said. He turned to the radio operator who'd come with Updike. "Patch a call through to the Riverlands Oil Company headquarters in Ashland, Kentucky and check it out."

The young man nodded.

"Meanwhile," Bolan went on, "we'll slow down and drift past that dock. If there's a barge full of dynamite waiting for us over there, somebody's going to be frustrated."

Following that suggestion, Tolliver brought the *Muldoon* almost to a stop. With the propellers turning slowly in reverse, the tow moved downstream even a little slower than the current.

ON MUSKRAT ISLAND, Sako Takahashi crouched at the edge of the water, in the cover of willow brush, and watched the *Henry J. Muldoon*.

The Japanese was clothed at last, in black combat fatigues. A naked man couldn't easily carry a soldier's weapons and ammo. He didn't carry one of the Uzi carbines he'd issued the others. The late Kurt Steiner had come to the island carrying the latest model of Ingram submachine gun. Takahashi knew a good weapon when he saw one, and he'd appropriated the Ingram for himself after Steiner was killed.

His side arm, hanging under a flap in a brown leather holster that had been lovingly cared for with saddle soap and oil, was a Nambu pistol. The automatic had been the standard issue for Japanese army officers from 1925 to 1945. Takahashi knew very well that the Nambu wasn't a first-class weapon, but the pistol had been carried by his grandfather, and it had special meaning. Sako had killed four men with it. His grandfather had used it to carry out eighteen executions.

Takahashi scowled at the towboat, which seemed to have stopped in the middle of the river. There was no way anyone on the *Muldoon* could have known that the barge wasn't there, so the tow should have been steering to the Ohio side.

The *Muldoon* wasn't responding to radio calls. That in itself was not significant, because Saladin had been ordered to prevent the captain from calling for help. He might have accomplished that by destroying the boat's radios, but it wasn't responding to light signals, either.

Maybe the fact that it was sitting almost dead still in the middle of the river was a signal.

There was only one way to find out.

"Shark! Come here. Take a boat and go out to see what's going on. Saladin's in charge. Tell him the plan has been changed and to continue moving slowly, while we transfer our explosives to one of the lead barges by boat."

Shark was one of the two other Japanese who served under Takahashi. He pointed at six men struggling to drag a boat across the island. Takahashi understood. The Shark would take the boat out to the *Muldoon* as soon as the men got it in the water.

When Gerd Keppler heard Takahashi's order and saw the Shark's response, he walked quietly away into the brush. As soon as he was out of sight from the Japanese, he trotted toward the riverbank.

The Shark joined the men dragging the boat, grunting orders to move faster. They took another five minutes to reach the bank and ease it down to the water. That done, the laborers turned back toward the island where there was more work to be done. The Shark settled into the tiny skiff and tried to start the motor.

Fifty years old and overweight, Keppler was neither quick nor agile. But this time he was fast enough. He sprang from the cover of brush and slammed the stainless-steel blade of a small hatchet into the Shark's skull. He didn't have to pull it out and strike a second time.

Keppler got in the boat, and after dumping the Shark into some reeds, pushed it out into the water. The outboard motor didn't start immediately, and he was seized with fear as he drifted past the spot where Takahashi had crouched at the top of the bank. Either the Japanese wasn't looking, or it was too dark for him to see who the man in the boat was.

The outboard started at last. Keppler steered for the *Henry J. Muldoon* until he was out of range of fire from Muskrat Island. He came close enough to the big towboat to see that it wasn't under the control of Saladin. There were no friendly greetings from its decks. Men stood around with weapons in their hands. When Keppler noticed that they wore camouflage suits, he knew immediately that they were American soldiers.

Keppler advanced the throttle and raced away up the river, throwing his Uzi and pistol overboard. He wouldn't be caught with illegal weapons, and if he had to answer questions when he went ashore, he had his driver's license as Benjamin Johnson. He was carrying plenty of cash in a money belt and the keys to a car he'd left parked on the street in Marietta two days earlier.

The Green and Black had failed. Sako Takahashi was too much the fanatic to admit it, but it was true. He would stay on Muskrat Island and probably die there. Gerd Keppler was of a more practical turn of mind.

"WONDER WHAT THAT was all about," Tolliver mused as he watched the skiff speed away up the river.

Bolan had been searching the island with binoculars for the past ten minutes.

"I just saw a light," he said. "That's the third one. There's somebody on that island."

"One guy less than there was five minutes ago," Tolliver said, nodding upriver toward the retreating skiff.

"What's on that island," Updike said, "is a bunch of guys with heavy weapons and a bunker full of explosives."

"There's only one way to find out for sure," Bolan stated.

"You mean by going ashore," Updike said. "That will be damned dangerous."

"That depends on how we do it."

A BOAT WAS PUT OVER the opposite side of the *Muldoon*, where Takahashi wasn't likely to see. It was a black rubber boat, and the Executioner occupied it by himself. With swift powerful paddle strokes he moved toward the shadows of the Ohio shoreline, then down the river.

When he was almost to the downstream end of the island, he paddled across. He let the current carry him a little beyond the end, and then paddled up the West Virginia side of Muskrat Island, keeping close to shore and in the shadows of trees and brush.

Bolan moved quietly, knowing that if he was seen, a burst or two of fire would do him in. Coming to a fallen tree, still attached by the bank, he decided this was a good place to go ashore. He tied the rubber boat to the tree and worked his way along the trunk to the land.

Besides the Calico M-900—reloaded with a full hundred rounds—he carried the Desert Eagle, the

Bali-Song knife, some rope and a radio, which he'd agreed to carry on his belt.

Climbing the bank, he found himself in deep woods where the moonlight didn't penetrate. It was choked with brush, and most of the trees were stunted by crowding. It was the kind of place where he'd fought many times before. The battle zone was as familiar to him as the back of his hand.

He crouched for a time and listened. Then, when he was reasonably confident no one was within earshot, he switched on the radio.

"Belasko's ashore."

"So's McGraw, Mike," Updike replied.

"What?"

"He went in on the lower end about half an hour ago. He took out two sentries. Maybe that's why you could get on the island without being shot at."

"Can I talk to him?"

"Only by relaying through me. He's on a different set of frequencies—police frequencies."

"Tell him I'm in thick woods on the West Virginia side, maybe half a mile from the downstream end. Tell him not to move."

"Fat damn chance he'll follow that order."

"If he has to move, tell him to go up the Ohio side. I don't want us to be shooting at each other."

"Roger."

"KEPPLER IS A TRAITOR!" Takahashi raged to Fitzgerald. "He must die! If nothing else is done, Keppler must die!"

In the moonlight where they stood, Fitzgerald let Takahashi see a sneer. "You want me to take a boat and go after him?"

"Then I'd never see either one of you again. Look at the boat. Saladin has failed and now I need you here to fight."

Fitzgerald looked at the *Henry J. Muldoon*, which stood almost still. If anything, it was backing upstream very slowly. "You ever think about hauling ass out of here?" he asked. "We're in deep shit, man."

Takahashi smiled bitterly. "You think I'm a fool? Of course I mean to escape from here. But not now. They're all around. We must wait for the confusion of battle. Then..."

"Why do you tell *me* this?" Fitzgerald asked skeptically.

"Some men," Takahashi said quietly, "are born to lead, to do great things. Most are meant to live futile little lives, then die." Takahashi's mouth twisted into an ugly smile. "I accept you into my class, Fitzgerald. You and I are going to survive."

"In which class did you put Keppler?" Fitzgerald asked.

Takahashi's eyes turned hard. "By turning traitor and running, he has preserved his miserable existence for a little while. He'd have been useless in battle, and I expected some betrayal from him. He had but an hour or less to live when—"

"Maybe he figured that out."

Sako Takahashi turned down the corners of his mouth. "Those meant to die are sometimes sly," he said. "But remember this—the more we kill, the easier our escape. If we sow terror among our enemies when they move, their fear and confusion will be our salvation."

BOLAN CONTINUED TO MOVE inland on the island. If there were sentries watching the river, he'd simply bypass them. Moving upstream through the tangled woods, he quickly covered distance without making much noise and without encountering anyone.

Eventually he came upon the brick foundation of what once had apparently been a house. A tiny dim red light appeared on his radio. He knelt, held it to his ear and switched it to receive.

"Where are you, Mike?"

"Tell McGraw that I just passed the ruins of a house and what might be a barn."

"Let me pass that on. Stand by."

Bolan waited a short time, until Updike returned. "He says you're about halfway up the island. From here on, things get hotter."

"Right. Where's Jack?"

"On the Ohio side, like you told him. Not as far up as you are. He says it's tough going."

"It *is*. Tell him to rest a few minutes. Out."

This was good. The father behind McGraw was in moving up the island, the more useful he'd be. The warrior moved out again, making his way through the woods at an even quicker pace.

When he knew he had to be coming close, Bolan stopped and checked his weapons. When the M-900 wasn't in use, the spring tension on the magazine could be released, saving the spring for better reliability.

Bolan made sure the spring was wound, then checked the Desert Eagle.

Confident that the tools for battle were ready, the Executioner headed out again.

Then he heard voices ahead of him. One voice in particular was shrill, angry and demanding.

The warrior knelt and activated the radio.

"Tell McGraw to get down under cover and let fly ten or fifteen rounds. Anything he's got that makes noise. Then move in. Jack's going to draw attention, so support him."

"You got it."

The warrior didn't have long to wait. McGraw had gotten the message quickly. From somewhere to Bolan's left and behind, the cracks of a high-caliber rifle were followed by the whine of ricocheting slugs.

Bolan listened carefully to the voices ahead of him.

"Move! Move! They're coming in! Down there!"

The voices were followed by the sound of men running recklessly through the brush.

Bolan moved again. Where was their damned bunker?

TAKAHASHI WATCHED with satisfaction as the boats moved away from the *Henry J. Muldoon*. So, they'd chosen their invasion beach, so to speak. Good. When they met more and better resistance than they'd figured, the terror and confusion would begin.

He'd sent ten men to fire on the boats, and one man to call in the sentries. The island was nearly two miles long, and they'd never all return in time to make much difference, but that was fine.

Everyone would be engaged, and the Ohio side of the island would be full of gunfire and confusion. Takahashi had a sinister smile on his face as he thought how easy it would be to slip off the West Virginia side of the island . . . and swim.

ALL HELL DID ERUPT on the Ohio side, as the Justice Department combat team's boats approached. They came under heavier fire than anyone could have expected.

The light on the little radio blinked urgently, and Bolan knew why. He could hear the sounds of the battle.

"We're getting shot to pieces!" Updike screamed into the radio. "More fire than—"

"Then back off," Bolan told him. "Fire on their muzzle-flashes."

He rose and sprinted through the woods toward the Ohio side. This wasn't how he wanted it to go, but the guys in the boats were in trouble. It didn't leave him much choice.

Bolan arrived at a point where the island was only a hundred yards wide. In a couple of minutes, he was directly behind the line of terrorists firing on the boats. They'd run recklessly to the top of the bank on the Ohio side of the island, never dreaming anyone could be behind them.

Bolan spotted three immediately. He leveled the M-900 and pulled the trigger.

He got two. The third man threw himself over the bank as soon as he heard the fire.

On the ground, alert and watching, Bolan looked for more gunners. Their fire had stopped for the moment, as they realized they had a problem behind them and took cover.

The Executioner activated his radio. "Okay! Let them have it!"

From far out on the water, the men in the boats loosed heavy fire at the shore. They were too far out to be effective, even if they were firing M-16s. But they gave the terrorists something to think about, which made it easier for Bolan to move forward.

He almost stepped on one guy who was crawling backward, retreating in panic from the kind of automatic-weapons' fire he'd never before encountered. When he realized he faced an enemy, he rolled over and raised the muzzle of the Uzi that Takahashi had issued to him less than an hour earlier.

Bolan drove the Bali-Song into his throat before he could get off a shot.

The Executioner crawled forward, aware now that he was on top of a gang of senseless killers.

When he heard the crack of McGraw's rifle, he cursed silently.

"Jack! Hang back! We got them from two sides!"

"Nothing like three!" replied the sheriff, who continued to fire.

Two gunmen trotted toward Bolan and dropped, cut down by a short burst from the M-900.

The men in the boats had regrouped and once again opened up a concentrated fire. It would have threatened Bolan if he hadn't expected it and kept close to the ground. They were below him on the water, and their fire could hit only a man who stood.

Except those who were below the lip of the river-bank. Or in the trees. It was possible that the barrage from the river had gotten some, but Bolan couldn't tell for certain.

"Jack! This is under control! Hang tight and clean up!"

"Yeah, sure."

Bolan wasn't confident that McGraw would abide by that order, but he moved out. There were things to do besides protect McGraw and the Feds in the boats.

IAN FITZGERALD HADN'T believed a word Takahashi said about being in an equal class and escaping together. But the Japanese didn't really care.

The whole scheme was coming down pretty much the way he'd figured it would. Every single element of it had failed. The tons of explosives in the bunker might as well be tons of sand, since they couldn't be moved. The lawmen would eventually take the island, and the damned warrior was still out there somewhere.

The time had come to move.

Takahashi tore off his black dungarees and threw aside the Ingram submachine gun. With the Nambu pistol strapped to his torso and a small cloth bag of throwing stars hanging around his neck, he strode into the middle of his former encampment. The place that had promised him great things now revealed only defeat. He cast his eyes upward and cursed the ghosts of all his life's failures.

And there Fitzgerald found him.

"Christ . . ."

Fitzgerald misunderstood Takahashi. He'd supposed there would be a word between them, as there would have been between any two civilized men. He didn't guess that the Japanese would just shove forward the muzzle of that antique pistol and fire a fatal shot.

He stood, legs spread, in the middle of his encampment, just outside his bunker, and listened to the firing on the Ohio side of the island. It was now or never.

Naked, ready to swim, he carried with him only his weapons and a small, sealed plastic bag containing $150,000. Even a naked man would find what he wanted when he handed someone a large amount of money.

But there was something more.

Takahashi was no fool. For a long time he'd had known that he'd eventually be betrayed. When the Semtex arrived, he'd fashioned a time bomb in the bunker.

The blast wouldn't only kill his enemies but would also cover his escape.

Takahashi walked down into the dark bunker, feeling his way through a chamber he knew all too well. He found the time device in the dark and activated it.

Now for the river . . .

THE EXECUTIONER WALKED directly across the top of the bunker, without realizing what it was. Only when he came to the abrupt drop that was the entrance did he comprehend and jump off to the side.

Takahashi saw the man Steiner had called the Devil.

The Japanese had confronted this man before and had a different name for him. He knew that before him was the man who'd martyred the leaders of Red Sword. What an honor to kill him!

And with the Nambu pistol. How appropriate!

BOLAN DIDN'T BELIEVE that either the encampment or the bunker had been abandoned. The terrorists had fought and were still fighting—to protect it. So he had jumped down equally to get away from an exposed place as in anticipation of hostiles.

Bolan was correct in his assumption. Takahashi wasn't the only man left in the clearing to defend the bunker. He'd kept two of his most trusted men.

One of them let fly a burst of 9 mm slugs in the general direction of the man who'd jumped down from the roof of the bunker. It wasn't the carefully aimed gunfire of a soldier, but with Takahashi in the vicinity, he was afraid not to fire, for fear the Japanese would suspect him of dereliction.

The burst was useful to the Executioner, however, who now had a target. The warrior matched the burst with one of his own, the difference being that Bolan's was accurate and cut the man almost in two.

Takahashi held his Nambu pistol in front of him as he swayed back and forth, looking for a chance to fire on the black-clad man. Few men deserved to die as much as this one, thought the Japanese. He had ruined the mission and he was probably also the man who had destroyed Red Sword.

Takahashi knelt in the sand and took aim with his pistol.

He had the devil in his sights. Carefully, gently, he squeezed the trigger.

But all he heard was a "click."

The Nambu had done the same thing before. For fifty years it had sometimes misfired. No matter. To kill this man with the old weapon was an honor, the misfire only added to it. And if he couldn't kill his great enemy with this special pistol, he'd find some way to keep him close to the bunker until his bomb detonated.

Takahashi grabbed back the slide and ejected the round. After rechambering another slug, he raised the pistol and took aim again.

But his prey had moved.

BOLAN HADN'T HEARD the click of the Nambu pistol but had moved off into the edge of the woods because he knew someone else had to be in the area. Under the cover of a thick stunted tree, he caught sight of... a naked man.

The warrior's mind raced. Although he didn't know his face, Bolan was sure it was Takahashi. That was how the Japanese terrorist fought.

Then he caught sight of a second man.

Tichiro Hirayama was thirty-two years old and bore the scars of a life of terrorism. His face revealed the vicious blows he'd received from police batons, and his lungs were seared by tear gas. Hirayama was a man driven by hate, all the more vengeful, since Takahashi had told him who the black-clad warrior was likely to be.

Although he shared similar ideals with Takahashi and had fought with him many times, Hirayama wasn't the type of man to discard an effective weapon in exchange for a rusty old pistol, no matter how "honored" he might think it was.

Hirayama picked up the Ingram that Takahashi had cast aside. He'd seen Takahashi aim at the man in black and not fire. He didn't care why. *He* would get the warrior in black—whether there was honor or not.

But Bolan was alert for someone else. He'd seen Takahashi move back into the woods before he had a chance to take him out. He searched now for any signs of other hostiles, unaware of the timer running in the bunker.

Tichiro Hirayama knew nothing of the timer, any more than Bolan did. He'd seen where the black-clad warrior edged into the woods, and he crouched on the roof of the bunker, Ingram aimed, watching for the least sign of movement.

Takahashi knelt in a tangle of brush, watching intently. For a moment he regretted having thrown away the Ingram so contemptuously. But, as he rubbed the old steel of the Nambu pistol, he satisfied himself that there was something spiritual between him and his grandfather's side arm.

Then he noticed someone crawling up the side of the bunker.

Takahashi squinted into the darkness, relieved only slightly by the moonlight that filtered down through the trees. He aimed the Nambu pistol, then closed his eyes and called on the spirit of his grandfather to help him. He adjusted his aim, pulled the trigger—

And killed Tichiro Hirayama.

Bolan heard the crack of the pistol, then saw a man five yards away stagger and fall. He swung the muzzle of the M-900 toward the woods and swept the area with three quick bursts. Takahashi was hit in both legs above the knees. He was perplexed, because he was convinced that his last shot had killed the black-clad warrior. Why, then, was Hirayama firing on him now? It made little difference. Even if it had been an accident, Hirayama had served his purpose.

The Japanese knelt and took aim on where he'd seen the last muzzle-flash. He was a little unsteady from his bloody wounds, but he steeled himself and concentrated.

Then he detected movement in the woods.

He still didn't know it was Bolan. The Executioner never stayed in one place after firing, and he was now moving through the brush trying to find his target.

Takahashi fired, not knowing that he'd missed Bolan by at least three feet. Crazed with his failure and pain, the Japanese terrorist had believed that once again the spirit of his dead grandfather had guided his hand.

Even so, he took no chances. He thrashed off through the brush toward the West Virginia side of the island. Just short of the water, he threw himself on the ground and examined his wounds with the tips of his fingers. They were only superficial. Now was the time for patience. Now was the time to wait.

The Executioner heard the thrashing in the brush come to an abrupt halt. He suspected that Takahashi was hit and acting irrationally. But with him irrational was no less dangerous.

Bolan trotted as quietly as he could toward the same side of the island. Behind him, he could hear the heavy fire of the fight between the Feds in the boats and the rest of Takahashi's gang. But here it was quiet. The malevolent Japanese terrorist was somewhere close, lying in wait in the brush. Bolan was cautious. He knew he faced an instinctive jungle fighter.

He dropped to his hands and knees, to make the lowest target possible, and waited, listening. After a couple of seconds, Bolan thought he heard the sound of breathing in front of him. He picked up a rotten limb that lay on the ground and tossed it in the direction of the sound.

Something smacked into the trunk of the tree just above him. Bolan reached up and felt for it, recognizing a throwing star instantly.

Two could play at that game. Bolan also knew how to use the ancient Japanese weapon, and he flipped it through the brush in the direction from where it came. He couldn't tell what it hit, if anything, but that wasn't the point. He had to draw Takahashi from his cover.

Another throwing star whipped through the air, this one landing in the trunk of a tree just inches from him.

The Executioner had had enough. He hugged the ground and loosed a storm of 9 mm rounds low across the ground. It was followed almost instantly by a blast, and the whine of a slug.

That gave Bolan a better idea where his man was. He leveled the M-900 in the direction from which the shot had come and fired a burst.

A man grunted.

Then Bolan heard the wild, desperate noise of a man thrashing through the woods, running in spite of whatever was behind him. Then he heard a splash. Takahashi had thrown himself into the river.

Bolan plunged down the bank after him. He knew he could be a little less cautious now, since the man could hardly shoot back if he was swimming. As the warrior reached the edge of the water, he saw Takahashi fifteen or twenty yards out, swimming clumsily. Bolan doubted the man could swim very far, but it was a chance he wasn't about to take. The Executioner raised the M-900 and aimed.

Then suddenly, the earth heaved up with a shock that hit Bolan like an enormous uppercut fist and threw him like a doll into the air and out over the water. He came down head first, stunned and disoriented. For half a minute he struggled to keep his head above water. It felt and looked as though the entire island—trees, brush, rock, sand—was in the sky overhead, hurled up in a dazzling eruption of light and sound.

After fighting not to sink and drown, Bolan then had to dive as deep as he could to avoid the bombardment of debris that fell on the surface of the river. He stayed down as long as he could, and when he came up it was still falling. He drew a deep breath and went down again. When he broke the surface of the water again, there was only light stuff falling.

He could see nothing of anyone. For a long moment it was as though he were the only man left alive on earth.

EPILOGUE

Muskrat Island was almost blown apart. The deep crater left after the blast filled quickly with water, because it was below the level of the river. Then the West Virginia edge of the crater crumbled and opened a channel to the river.

The body of Sako Takahashi was found in a tangle of willows along the shore, half a mile down the island. He'd bled heavily from wounds, but the immediate cause of death was drowning. Eighteen governments issued statements announcing themselves gratified to know he was dead.

Enough was found of the body of Ian Fitzgerald to identify him. Four governments were pleased by that.

Part of another body was found hanging in a tree, but there wasn't enough to determine who the man had been. One of the men captured after the firefight on the Ohio side of the island mentioned Tichiro Hirayama, but they couldn't be sure. He remained on the wanted list.

Nine of the Green and Black gunners who'd been firing on the boats had died in the battle. Sheriff Jack McGraw had picked off four of them with his rifle. The survivors, including some wounded, were rounded up after the explosion.

Some of the identifications were intensely interesting to law enforcement agencies all over the world. The list was almost like a "Who's Who" of international terrorism. One of the bodies was that of the "student revolutionary" who had bombed a university laboratory. The Marine deserter surrendered and was shortly picked up by SPs from the Corps. The Japanese known as "The Shark", whose body was found on the Ohio side of the island, was identified as the man who'd brought down a Korean airliner with a Semtex bomb.

Saladin, the man killed aboard the *Henry J. Muldoon* by Donna Dow, turned out to be a Palestinian wanted for the murder of eleven Israeli schoolchildren. They'd died when he ignited a gasoline bomb in their school cafeteria.

Gerd Keppler wasn't found. Some of the captured men said he'd been on the island, but no one knew where he'd gone.

None of the federal officers or the local officers were killed. They'd been fighting almost a mile away from the explosion. Six men had been wounded in the firefight, one seriously.

Jasmin al-Said, after a short stay in a Washington hospital, was delivered to the Qatari embassy by representatives of Marietta College. She wasn't awarded a degree, but was given a certificate attesting to her "excellent character and scholarship" during her period as a college student.

Donna Dow accepted an offer from Riverlands Oil Company to stay aboard the *Henry J. Muldoon*. Lisa was retiring soon, and Donna decided she could hardly find a more suitable place to work. Captain Tolliver had made a special effort to let the company know what she'd done.

MOST OF THIS OCCURRED after the Executioner was long gone from the Ohio Valley.

He'd stumbled ashore, stunned by the concussion of the blast, and had climbed the bank to stare at the huge smoking crater that was already filling with water. The first man to reach him was Jack McGraw. Fearing he'd be caught in the cross fire of the Green and Black and the lawmen in the boats, he'd retreated to a section of the island that was relatively unscathed by the blast. When he found the big warrior, he threw his arms around him and actually wept.

Bolan left the island in the next half hour, first by boat to the *Henry J. Muldoon*, then by boat again to Marietta, and finally by car to the farmhouse.

Donna was with him when he arrived. She'd obviously fallen for him, and it was with some pain—and a little awkwardness—that he explained the impossibility of any kind of lasting relationship. Although a little hurt, she was quick to understand. Besides, she had an exciting new career ahead of her.

Their goodbye was cut short by Brad Updike, who brought an urgent message from Hal Brognola. The Executioner's presence was required in Wonderland immediately. A government jet would be waiting for him within the hour so that he could be briefed on his next mission.

"I'd have thought they'd give you at least twenty-four hours," the Justice Department man said as he handed Bolan the message.

"The other side doesn't give *us* twenty-four hours," the Executioner replied.

From the publishers of AGENTS, an action-driven new miniseries focusing on the war against drugs.

CODE ZERO

D. A. HODGMAN

The action gets hot when CENTAC—an elite tactical unit of the DEA—receives CODE ZERO. The license to track and terminate, CODE ZERO is the DEA's answer to the drug cartels.

In Book 1: SPEEDBALL, DEA agents are massacred in a furious firefight, but one is kept alive and taken hostage. Agent Harry Wolfe will stop at nothing to rescue her as he battles against the rampaging gunmen.
